D1756108

Slipping Through

Journey into different dimensions

A Collection of Other World Tales

Miranda Kate

Notes from the Author

The two short stories in Slipping Through, InterDimensioning and V.W.G, were initially created as serialised flash fiction entries written for photo prompts. But the novella, The Game, comes from a novel I wrote, which in its original incarnation was called The Jester.

I started it in 1991, the idea sparked by the office manager I sat opposite in my first job – Mr Gilbert. He laughed one day and the Jester was born.

The first draft took seven years to write, and a second draft even got sent out to publishers two years later – much to my shame now, particularly after unearthing many plot holes in it during a creative writing course a couple of years later. I shelved it for a good decade and a half until it got dusted off to use as fodder for more flash stories. I thought I could lift pieces out but it needed too much work, so I wrote fresh pieces, exploring the characters and ideas a little deeper.

Still liking the story and its concept I decided to put it together as a novella and publish it. And so here it is for your delight.

People have asked many questions about the origins of the Jester – who is he, where does he come from? And the girls, Isabella and Annie, what's their story? As yet I haven't uncovered it, but spending time with them again has provided some ideas, so a potential future sequel is gestating.

Dedication

For Eddie Fargnoli & Mark Jordan
Whose cries of 'we want more' back
in 1990 encouraged me on.

Contents

InterDimensioning

Chapter 1

Elise thought she was seeing things. She rubbed her eyes. Nope, it was purple - or lilac - of all different shades. She turned a full circle taking in the hills around her and the strange growths that covered them, which she supposed were trees, despite their colour. She had never seen yellow bark before. She checked her watch, but it didn't tell her anything. No time had passed as she knew it wouldn't here. In fact, if she waited it might even start moving backwards. She sighed. She was sick of these games and she didn't want to play anymore.

She sat down cross-legged on the soft grass – the only thing that appeared normal. She wondered how long Logan would be. She didn't fancy hanging around here for too long; she felt exposed.

Scanning the hills, she felt like her ears were reaching out to pick up any unusual sounds, but there was nothing out of sync, there were only normal wildlife noises like bird song, the shuffling of small creatures, and wind through the trees. If it wasn't for their odd colour, she would've thought she'd been transported to another place in her own dimension.

She tapped her watch. Yes, it was still working, the second hand was moving. She had expected something freakier, like last time, especially after Logan's description. Although when she remembered how he'd described that place - the entire underestimation (they'd had to run for their lives to the portal) - she figured that maybe this time he was overcompensating just to be on the safe side.

She was also learning that his perception was a little off kilter. He looked at things as though he could see round corners – and maybe he could. I mean, how many people could just move someone out of their own dimension in a blink of an eye? Not many. Most of them had some kind of giant machine in their house to do it, and even then the chances of finding anything interesting were slim.

Logan had developed such a simple method with the tiny doorway he'd built. He'd snap his fingers and they were gone. If others found out it could destroy the entire portal industry, but wasn't that how it had happened with computers? They used to fill rooms with machines to get just one tiny megabyte, and now you could attach a screen to your wrist to access and store everything.

This thought prompted Elise to look at her watch again. How long was he going to be?

She heard a loud sucking pop behind her, and stood up. Finally.

But the look of alarm on his face as he ran towards her quenched her impatience.

"Quick Elly! RUN!"

A crunching sound was following him and the entire hill behind him shifted. The lilac trees were starting to blend together. She didn't need to ask what was happening; she'd journeyed with Logan through dimensions enough times to know how dangerous it could be. She reached out and grabbed his hand as he passed and they ran together into what she hoped was an exit.

Chapter 2

They dove into the closest lilac trees, the crunching sound behind them softening until it stopped all together. It became so dark that Elise couldn't decide if they had gone through another portal or not. The only thing visible was a circle of light in front of them. It grew into an opening. They stepped through and discovered a road.

Elise could have believed they'd arrived back home had it not been for the lilac trees that lined it. The trucks and cars parked along it wouldn't have been out of place in her hometown. But the silence around them spoke of something different.

Elise's grip on Logan's hand tightened as they began walking. Logan pulled her into the middle of the road, his eyes scanning the trees with suspicion.

They were travelling uphill and when they reached the rise of the road they were greeted with a breathtaking sight: a wide expanse of sea lay in front of them, its waters meeting brilliant white sand. They paused.

"Do you think it's safe?" Elise asked.

Logan shrugged. "There's only one way to find out."

They continued to walk until the tarmac petered out and the sand took over. They made their way to the water's edge and stood looking out over it. Logan's head was bowed and Elisa wondered what he was doing. He seemed to be studying the water. She lifted her foot to dip the toe of her shoe into it when he shot out a hand to stop her. She turned to him about to speak, but his finger was on his lips, and he whispered, "Look and listen."

She stared at the water and waited, but she heard nothing. Then she realised what he meant: there was no sound, no whoosh as the water moved back and forth no matter how big the wave. Then she observed the motion of the water. It wasn't really back and forth – it was rising and falling.

"Is it water? What is it?" she hissed.

"I don't know, but I wouldn't touch it if I was you."

Elise reached down to pick up a small rock next to her right shoe. She glanced at Logan to see if he was watching. She showed him the stone and brought her arm back ready to throw it. He gave a slight nod of approval, so she launched it high into the air.

There was a faint 'plop' as it hit the surface, but there was no splash or ripple. They looked at each other wide-eyed.

But then the water did move. It began to retract from the sand, drawing back and gaining height. Logan grabbed Elise's hand again and stepped back, not daring to take his eyes off the growing mass. Elise moved with him. Her breath caught in her lungs as her mind reeled at what she might have unleashed. But just as they thought they were going to have to run a second time, the water stopped. And then something hit Elise square in the chest.

She let out a startled cry and looked at the ground to see what it was; it was the rock she had thrown. She picked it up and stared at it in amazement, finding the same shock on Logan's face when she turned to him.

The mass returned to its water-like state and resumed its wave motion as though nothing untoward had taken place.

They backed up further without saying a word, not daring to turn their backs on whatever was in front of them until they were at a safe distance. Once they felt tarmac under their feet they paused.

"What now Logan, what are we going to do now? We can't go back, it's not safe, but neither is what's in front of us."

Logan pulled a square box out of his pocket and started fiddling with it. "I don't think we should explore this dimension any further." He looked up, his eyes flitting about them. "There are clearly things here that are beyond our understanding. If the trees and the seas aren't to be trusted, I wonder at those cars."

Elise glanced over her shoulder at the parked cars and trucks. It hadn't occurred to her that they might not be what they seemed.

Logan held the box out in front of him and drew a door in the air.

"Where are we going then?"

"Home."

Elise glanced at her watch. "But it's too soon; it won't be there yet, not as we know it. Remember the time loop?"

Logan grinned. "Well we can find out what will be there."

Elise baulked. "Logan, that's taking an awfully big risk."

"Every dimension jump is a risk Elise. Come on, you wouldn't be here if you didn't want adventure."

He held out his hand. She paused for one more second before taking it, and together they stepped through the outline in the air.

Chapter 3

When they stepped out onto the densely packed pine needles that made up the floor of what appeared to be a forest, Elise was confused.

"This isn't home."

Logan was busy studying the box in his hand, his brow furrowed.

"No, it's not. I couldn't bring us straight there because it doesn't exist as we know it yet." He looked up at the trees around them. "But this wasn't the plan either; I didn't envisage a forest being here."

They heard a crunching sound deep among the trees. Elise stepped closer to Logan. They peered round waiting. Then another noise came from the other side of the forest, higher pitched, like metal being cut. Their heads spun round in that direction. Logan clasped Elise's hand ready to run, but it stopped as abruptly as it started.

"Logan, where are we?" Elise whispered.

"I don't know," he hissed back through clenched teeth. "I'm trying to work it out."

His fingers stabbed at the buttons on the box following a rhythm. Then they stopped.

"Oh God."

Logan's tone prompted a sinking feeling in Elise's stomach. "What?"

"Shit." Logan's face looked pale as he started to frantically jab at the buttons again.

"What? What is it Logan?" Elise struggled to control the rising panic she felt.

"I thought I'd programmed the portal to take us back into our dimension and I did, but ..." He stared at the LED panel on the box for a second before punching the buttons again.

"But what?" Elise hissed urgently.

"I made a miscalculation."

"So where are we?"

He looked at her, the beads of sweat on his forehead highlighting the fear in his eyes. The hairs on her forearms prickled.

"You know how they say each dimension has a parallel where things run on a different premise to ours?" Elise nodded. "It's seems I've landed us right in one."

A crease fluttered across Elise's forehead, but it was broken by another crunching sound, this time a lot closer. She grabbed for Logan, and he grabbed back.

"I don't understand Logan, what does that mean?"

Logan pocketed the box and brought his arm round Elise's shoulder drawing her in, not taking his eyes off the imposing pine trees circling them.

"It means that in this dimension Humans aren't the top of the food chain. This world is run by another species."

Elise studied his face, which was busy looking up studying the trees. She followed his gaze. "What species Logan?"

She saw the tops of the conifers move as though swaying to a breeze she couldn't feel. Then the crunching sound came again and this time more tree trunks appeared between those that were already there.

"The trees," he breathed.

"So let's get out of here!" Her eyes were wide with terror at the thought of what the trees could do.

"We can't."

Elise froze. "What? Why not?"

"I can't open a portal from a parallel."

"Why not?"

"It doesn't work the same way, I need a different machine."

"So what are you saying Logan, that we're stuck here?" Elise struggled to get her mind round the idea.

He swallowed, nodding at her. "I'm sorry I got you into this Elise."

"So am I."

They clutched each other as the trees moved closer, the crunching sound escalating until their minds were full of it. Then the high pitched noise started up again and they gritted their teeth, burying their faces in each other's necks until they didn't know anything anymore.

Chapter 4

Elise blinked, but it didn't make any difference, she still couldn't see anything. She heard a shuffle next to her, and then a hand on her knee reassured her that Logan was still with her. She was sitting upright, but she couldn't work out where. The smell of earth was pungent and when she touched the ground it felt cold and damp, leaving moist bits on her hand.

"Where are we?" she whispered.

"I don't know." Logan squeezed her leg and shuffled closer, bringing his arm round her. She was glad of the comfort.

"How long were we out for?"

"No way of telling, but I'm glad that we're still together."

"Me too." Elise snuggled into him.

A shuffling sound reached their ears and a pinprick of light appeared. As it grew larger it lit up their surroundings. They were in an underground cavern that had tree roots running all round the walls and floor.

As the light approached they saw it was a hollow ball of twisted twigs or roots, carried by a long vine with a firefly trapped inside. Behind it were two other vines carrying leaves which were placed on the ground in front of them, along with the light. The vines retracted and Elise and Logan sat up to take a closer look.

Logan reached out his hand to touch one of the leaves. It unfolded to reveal collections of different coloured berries. He glanced at Elise who shrugged.

"Food?"

"They're feeding us? Why?" Logan picked up a red berry and sniffed it, then passed it to Elise.

She turned it over in her fingers. "Do you think they're poisonous?"

"If they wanted us dead they would have killed us already."

"True." Elise nibbled at an edge while Logan watched her. She licked her lips. "It's sweet, try it." Logan picked one up and tentatively bit into it.

After they had tasted one of each colour, they took in their surroundings.

Elise said, "What now? Should we try crawling out?"

Logan shrugged. Then a voice cut across the cavern, making them both jump.

"I wouldn't if I were you."

They could just make out a shape across the dark space. They heard a scraping sound and a figure crawled into view. Its movements were stilted and as it came closer they realised that it wasn't human, although it was clearly designed to look like one; the eyes gave it away with the mechanisms and cogs visible behind the translucent colouring.

"Who are you? And how did you get here?" Logan asked.

"I am Reginald, a data droid, left here by the last humans that passed through this world."

"Why did they leave you here?"

"They didn't have a choice, they died."

Elise felt her stomach clench.

"And why shouldn't we try and crawl out?" Logan ignored the droid's last statement.

"Because it's too small and they won't let you stay outside."

"They?"

"The trees."

"Why?"

"I'm not entirely sure, but when my humans tried it, they kept being returned to this same cavern over and over again."

"And then what happened?"

The droid paused. "I'm not sure what you mean, sir. My humans kept trying until they became too weak and died."

This stopped Logan. Elise could see his mind working, his mouth opened a couple of times but nothing came. She pulled away from him slightly.

"How did you get into this world?" she asked.

"A malfunction in my programming; we were suppose to be going into the fifth."

"The fifth?"

"Another timeline besides our own that my humans liked to travel to for parties."

Logan's eyes lit up. He sat forward. "You're able to travel into other timelines?"

"Yes sir. But for some reason we ended up here … although I'm not sure where here is exactly."

"It's a parallel dimension: rather than moving forward or back into different dimensions we've gone sideways, entering one where other species dominate."

Reginald blinked, and a whirring could be heard, then he blinked again and said, "Excuse me. I'm not functioning at my best, having been in this damp cavern for some time. A parallel you say? My humans didn't consider that."

"Are you still malfunctioning?" Logan asked.

"My humans tried to correct my programming but they couldn't work out where we were, so they couldn't reroute us back."

"Would it be possible for me to try programming you?" Logan brought his hands out and wiggled his fingers.

"Are you familiar with data droids, sir?"

"Call me Logan. And no, not droids, we don't have any yet, but I do create programs for lots of other data machinery. Would you allow me to try?"

Reginald pressed a place on his torso, and a flap opened to reveal a numeric pad. Logan moved the firefly light in between them to take a closer look. He smiled.

"It's the same sort of keypad we use. With your help I might be able to work something out."

Chapter 5

Elise frowned at Logan's suggestion. "What? To try and get us out of here?"

"That's the plan. Why? Did you want to stay?" Logan half laughed at the idea.

"I'm just curious that's all. Why have the Trees put us here, and why are they feeding us?"

Reginald interjected, "Madam, I don't think they intend harm, but I don't think they have encountered our species before. The food they supplied for my two humans was woefully small."

"But isn't there a way to communicate with them?"

"I'm not a communication droid, so I have never tried."

"Did your humans try?"

"My humans just kept trying to escape. One of them had an extremely low tolerance for small spaces, so they would scrabble out. Then those noises would knock them out and they would be returned."

"But maybe those noises are their speech?"

"Elise, that doesn't help if it knocks us out every time," Logan snorted. He continued to press buttons on Reginald's keypad in a repetitive sequence.

They all heard a scraping sound from the other wall, and then the roots around them vibrated. Elise reached out a hand and touched one, snapping it back seconds later. "It's like an electric shock."

Logan touched another one and did the same. "More a static shock. Interesting."

"What do you think it means?" Elise said, rubbing her fingers.

"I really don't know, but I can't imagine we will ever find out."

They heard a rumbling sound and the earth started to move. They covered their heads and huddled together as pieces of mud and rocks started falling about them. They remained this way for some time, until there was one final shudder and everything stopped.

They slowly raised their heads - Elise spitting out bits of dirt that had landed on her lips. The fireflies were still with them and still working, so they could just make out something dark at the other end of the cave. Logan picked up one of the firefly balls and crawled over towards it.

"It's a hole, a big hole, big enough for us. And I can feel a breeze, I'm sure of it."

Elise joined him. "Do you think it's their way of inviting us out? Reginald has this happened before?" she called over her shoulder.

"No miss, although there was always a hole, just not really big enough for my humans. Maybe they are learning you need more space."

Elise looked at Logan. "Shall we go?"

"They seem to want us to. Come on Reginald."

"No Mr Logan, I think I'll stay."

"I'm not going without you Reginald, you're our ticket out of this dimension."

They heard a couple of blooping sounds before he spoke again. "I would always stay here; the humans didn't want to risk me getting broken on the climb out."

Logan looked at the size of the hole and at Reginald. "I think you'll fit, it depends if it narrows or not. Come on."

Reginald shuffled over to them and Logan led the way through the tunnel. It raised slightly as they went up, but eventually the light grew and they could see an opening at the end.

When they climbed out, they didn't expect what greeted them: other humans.

Chapter 6

The group of people standing in the clearing facing them looked ready for a film shoot, dressed as they were in old costumes from 1970s science fiction movies. A few of them appeared as different species and it was one of these that stepped forward.

But when the giant bear-like creature made a strange grunting sound, Elise couldn't stop herself from giggling. This seemed to cause confusion; the strange people looked at each other, worried expressions on their faces, but the bear gave another grunt and this time offered his paw.

Elise glanced at Logan. "What do you think it means?" she whispered.

Logan gave her round eyes and a shrug. "Beats me."

There was a shuffling at the back and something was passed from hand to hand until the bear took hold of what looked like a flower and proffered it to Elise.

Again she glanced at Logan. He said, "Take it." So she did with a smile and replied, "Thank you."

This seemed to work as the group all nodded at each other and gave off sounds of laughter.

Elise brought the flower to her nose. It looked like a sunflower, but the yellow seemed brighter, more vibrant. She stroked it with her finger and sniffed it. The circular way the seeds ran round its centre made it appear as though it was moving, like a wheel being turned. Elise watched it. Round and round they went, on and on with no end.

She heard a sound to her right where Logan was standing. He was speaking but she couldn't quite hear him. All she caught was "… fading, I can't see you, what's happening Elise?!"

She tried to turn her head but it wouldn't move, and the seeds just kept turning, round and round. She wanted to move her eyes from them but couldn't. Then a breeze hit her face and broke the spell.

The view shocked her. How did she get here? Where did this field come from? She spun round in a pirouette but she was alone, and all she could see right out to the horizon in every direction were green fields. No trees, no shrubs, just grass - long whispering grass.

And it was whispering. Something was being said, she was sure of it. She leaned down trying to hear, trying to make out the words. If she could just get a tiny bit closer she would be able to catch them, she was sure of it.

Suddenly she fell, tipping right over, her forehead hitting the ground – hard.

The world crowded in again and she could hear movement around her, lots of bodies and Logan's voice.

"Elise! Are you alright? What happened, you disappeared for a few seconds. Elise!"

He was at her side, pulling her up into a sitting position. She could feel a trickle of blood down her nose. She looked at him stunned. "Where am I?"

"You're here with us – me and Reginald, and … well whoever these people are, in the tree world. Remember?"

It came back to her and she looked round at their faces, at the group of science fiction movie characters. There was something not quite right, something odd: they were too staged, too deliberately dressed up.

She was still clutching the flower. She chucked it at them and shouted, "You're not real, are you? The trees made you up? What do you want from us?"

Shocked faces looked back at her, but then there was a shudder in the ground and a collective shimmer ran through the bodies before they winked out.

Logan breathed, "Oh my God they were a projection of some sort." He stepped forward and wafted his arms around the spaces they had inhabited. "How did they do it?"

Reginald gave off a couple of bleeps before saying, "Shouldn't we be asking why they did it? What were they trying to achieve?"

"I don't like this Logan, please try and get us out of here." Elise wiped her forehead and showed him the blood to emphasise her point.

"I will Elise, but where did you go when you sniffed that flower?"

"Fields, just open fields - of grass. I couldn't see any landmarks."

"But how?"

"Maybe some kind of hallucinogenic, Mr Logan. The trees would know all about the plant life here." Reginald pointed at the discarded flower.

"But her body actually physically vanished. That's like some kind of transportation device. Maybe we could use it? Or maybe they were offering us a way out?"

"Logan, we can't afford to mess about with some unknown device that could take us to God knows where. You said you thought you could reprogram Reginald, so let's stick with that."

Logan pulled Elise up onto her feet. "Yeah, you're right. I'm just curious that's all. It's a chance to explore."

"I'm bleeding Logan. I'm scared. I want to go home." Tears welled up in Elise's eyes.

"Okay, Elise. I'll see what I can do."

Logan turned to Reginald who had his keypad open and ready. He bent down and started punching in sequences again, across and round the keypad. More bleeping and staccato sounds were emitted. Then Logan stopped abruptly and stood up, taking a careful step backwards.

"Logan?" Elise didn't like his expression. "What is it? What's the matter?"

"Where are you really from, Reginald? What is your true purpose?" Logan's tone sent a chill through Elise; it was firm, but it had an edge, as though he'd uncovered something that scared him.

Reginald went through another series of bleeps and then stopped all movement. His eyes were open and directed at them, but they were no longer focused.

There was silence: nothing moved in the trees, nothing stirred – no wind, no signs of life. It scared Elise. She side stepped until she could feel Logan's arm against hers and whispered, "There's no sound – from anywhere."

Logan's eyes darted around the trees. The stiff movement of his head indicated his fear. Then Elise felt his hand slip into hers.

Chapter 7

The silence from the trees continued.

Elise whispered, "What happened with Reginald, what spooked you?"

He whispered back, "The codes I was programming into him should have changed the set up of the timelines, but they kept returning to those that brought us here. It's like he wanted us to remain here or something."

"What do you think it means?"

"I'm not sure. Maybe he's a device they're using to communicate with us."

"They?"

"The Trees. But I'm trying to work out what those holograms were about, and that flower. You said it took you to another place?"

"Yes, just for a moment. When I hit my head I came back though."

Logan searched the ground around their feet. The sunflower was still lying where Elise had thrown it. He moved away from her to pick it up.

"Logan what are you doing?" Elise hissed at him. The flower was face down. She could see his mind working. "What are you thinking?"

"Well let's assume that Reginald and the holograms were their way of communicating with us, and the flower did indeed lead us out of here."

"Okay. But why would they do that?"

"We are working on the assumption that the trees are bad and they want to hurt us, but are they?"

"I don't follow." Elise was confused. "Reginald told us about how the other humans had perished here."

"Yes, but he also told us that the trees gave them food, just not enough. And how the noise they made caused them to pass out each time – as it did with us when we arrived."

"Okay." Elise was beginning to see what he was getting at.

"So maybe they have devised another way to communicate with any unsuspecting humans that arrive here."

"What, by using a device that they left here?"

"Yes." Logan walked over to Reginald and tapped his shoulder. There was no movement; he remained in the same unmoving state. "He's real enough, not like the others."

Logan was still holding the flower. Elise pointed at it. "So what are you going to do with that?"

"Well maybe it's our way out of here. Maybe that's why they gave it to you. If we both go through to another place, maybe my box will work there to get us home?"

Elise gave Logan a dubious look.

"Elise, we've got nothing to lose at this point. Staying here really isn't an option."

She pulled a face, and said, "Okay. But we might be better off lying down first. I bent down to hear something, that's what made me fall."

"Let's give it a try." Logan lay down on the ground next to her and she joined him. He held her hand in one hand and the flower in the other, making sure it was over both of them so they could see it at the same time.

Within seconds of looking at the centre Elise could feel herself spinning again. She didn't resist it this time and before long she found herself in the field, with Logan at her side. He put the flower down and they both lay there for a few seconds as though waiting to see if they would stay. Nothing changed.

Slowly Logan sat up and pulled Elise with him. They looked round at the long grass waving in the breeze. There were no trees on any horizon. Logan stood up. Elise remained where she was.

"Aren't you coming?"

"Can you hear anything Logan?"

He frowned at her, cocking his head slightly. "Only the breeze through the grass."

"No whispering?"

"What are you talking about?"

She listened, but he was right, there was only the breeze in the grass. "Last time I thought I heard voices coming from the grass – but I couldn't quite hear what they were saying."

"Voices? Could it have been my voice from the other side?"

Elise hadn't considered that. She nodded. "Maybe."

Logan pulled the box from his pocket and looked at it. He punched in some numbers and his face lit up. "We're back in business."

Elise had never felt so overjoyed. She leapt to her feet. "We get to go home?"

"Yes. I'm not taking us anywhere else. I think we've had enough for a while."

Elise nodded.

Logan spent a few minutes punching in the numbers and then he took Elise's hand. "Ready?"

"Never been more so."

Logan pointed the box at the air next to them, and drew a rectangular shape. The air within it shifted, going a shade darker, and they stepped through together.

It was like climbing into a cupboard. When they stepped out the other side, they were in Logan's apartment. Relief filled Elise's heart, while Logan walked across the room and opened the French windows, stepping out onto the balcony. She joined him.

They looked out over the city, breathing in the late afternoon air.

"Nothing looks any different, I think we're home."

Logan stepped back inside and picked up a clock. "Yep, we've only been away about two hours."

Elise shook her head. "That always amazes me. It feels like we've been gone for days."

"This time round, definitely." They heard a scratching and a whine at the door. Logan opened it and his dog, Sunny, came bounding into the room, jumping up at them both, overjoyed to see them.

"Fancy coming with me to take Sunny for a walk?"

Elise took another breath of the afternoon air, and said, "Sure. It'll be a good way to wind down after all the stress."

Logan put a lead on Sunny and they exited the apartment, taking the road down to the park He kept glancing up. Elise followed his gaze.

"What you looking at?"

"The trees. I don't think I'll ever look at them the same way again!"

She laughed.

V.W.G

Part 1

Vladimir hoped his back tyre wouldn't slide again. He hated cycling in the snow, let alone at high speed. He needed to get to the professor fast, but ploughing through this stuff was making it hard. There wasn't much time left, not if what he had just discovered was true. He needed the professor to confirm it pronto.

His time at the Sternberg Astronomical Institute had sped up as they began to realise just how much of a prodigy he was. The professor had taken him under his wing, nurturing his ability to see things others couldn't in all the complicated theory. The professor had also made him aware that once word got out about him, others would want to use his talent for far less desirable purposes. Security had been tightened around him to prevent anyone approaching him – or worse, kidnapping him.

It was this that caused him to keep looking over his shoulder now. He had seen that black sedan before. It might look nondescript to others – and in Moscow they were a common enough sight – but with his photographic memory he knew exactly where the registration had come up before: both outside his house and at the professor's lab. Of course there were other residents that it could belong to in both those places, but the way this one was keeping its distance, randomly stopping and starting, raised his suspicions. And even though Vladimir had taken two short cuts through housing estates, it was still in view over his shoulder.

As he rounded the corner into the professor's street he was able to speed up, the road having been recently cleared of snow. He whizzed into the side alley by the main building and jumped off, dragging his bike out of sight into a doorway. He was sure the sedan would drive by the end of the alleyway in a second, but he didn't see it before he rushed into the side entrance and up the stairs to the professors' rooms.

He burst into the classroom, startling all the students, but when Professor Shustov saw his face, he didn't reprimand him. Instead he dismissed the class for the day and took Vladimir by the elbow, leading him out to his personal office.

"What is it Vlad? What have you found?"

"Oh professor, you have to check this for me, I can't be sure, but if I'm right we haven't got much time."

The professor took the proffered piece of folded paper and moved to his desk to pick up his glasses. "Much time for what, Vlad?"

"You remember we talked about proving the sim possibility? How it was only a matter of finding a glitch in the figures we ran on the parallel universe theories?"

"Yes?" The professor's eyes widened as Vladimir spoke, knowing that nothing he did was ever to be taken lightly.

"Well I found one – well two in fact, but I also found something else: that when they happen there is a way to switch them."

"Switch them? You mean we could run another reality, like changing train tracks?"

"Well more like a junction really, as I'm sure there are more possibilities. But I need you to check these figures, to see if they're right, so then we'll know when the next one will happen."

The professor paused. "What? We'll know exactly?"

"Yes."

The professor gawked at him for a second then fumbled the piece of paper open and rushed round to his chair, thumping down into it while picking up a pen.

There was silence while he looked it over. Vladimir felt like he was holding his breath as he watched the professor's pen follow the figures down the page. When it reached the end, the professor looked up at Vladimir with trepidation, his pen still sitting on the last figure.

"As I suspected, there's nothing incorrect here," he said in a low tone. "So tell me Vlad, how long have we got?"

"About two hours, Professor."

Vladimir thought the professor's eyes were going to pop out of his head. "Two hours?! But we'll never be ready that soon. How often are they occurring, surely we can wait for the next one."

"Well, that depends, Professor. From my calculations there won't be another for 30 years, will we both still be here then?"

The professor knew better than to question any of Vladimir's figures.

For a second he didn't move, then he sprang up and said, "There's no time to waste. We need to go now!"

He bundled his coat on as he left the room, Vladimir at his heels. They rushed out the main doors to the professor's four wheel drive and Vladimir noted the sedan parked across the street.

As he climbed into the front seat, he said, "I was followed here, Professor."

The professor glanced at the sedan as he reversed out. "I know Vlad, you've been shadowed for a couple of weeks now, but don't worry, they've only got a couple of hours left!" He chuckled, and Vlad chuckled with him as they sped off in the direction of the professor's home.

Part 2

The professor swung into his driveway, the garage door opening automatically. In the rearview mirror they both noticed the black sedan passing the house as the door closed behind them.

"What if we don't manage it? What shall I do about them?" Vlad glanced at the professor with fear in his eyes.

"One bridge at a time, Vlad, one bridge at a time. The question really is should we switch if we can?" The professor jumped down from the car and pressed the central locking while Vladimir joined him at the inner door to the house.

"But isn't that the whole point of doing this?"

The professor raised his eyebrows as he unlocked the door. "Yes, I suppose it is." They both tumbled into the kitchen and the professor started getting out some mugs.

"What are you doing, Professor?"

"Making cocoa."

"What?" Vladimir blinked, thinking he must have misheard him.

"You need to redo the figures so we know exactly how long we've got – to the second - and then we can synchronise clocks and do a countdown." He lit the gas burners on the hob. "And while you're doing that, I'll make some cocoa. I'm freezing." The professor rubbed his hands together and held them up to the gas burners.

Vladimir sat down on a stool at the kitchen counter and grabbed the pad and pencil lying there. He pulled out the paper he'd snatched up on their way out of the institute and started scribbling.

Just as the Professor poured the milk into the mugs, Vladimir turned round and said, "I've done it."

"Okay, when?"

"15:17."

"An hour and 15 from now?" The professor looked up at the kitchen clock and his wrist watch.

"Yes."

"Well come on then, let's go downstairs and get the computer clock synced too."

He took both mugs with him to a small door under the stairs. Vladimir followed and leaned forward to open it for him, flicking a switch on the right. The stairs came into view and the professor went down them, flicking another switch at the bottom with his elbow. The basement flooded with light, and he placed the drinks down on a huge desk that lined the right side wall before turning on the power to the computer.

"Have you any idea how it will show up, Vlad?"

"On the computer it'll show up in code - you'll need to run it in DOS - it should be easy to spot. But in the real world? I've no idea, Professor. It could be a minor change like a sensation, although if we switch, it should be a lot bigger."

The professor ran the computer in DOS and the three large screens displayed rows of figures and symbols, some with cursors and question marks at the end. Vladimir joined him and started typing in commands, causing large quantities of data to scroll across the screen. The professor winced at it. "Are you sure it'll be easy to spot, it looks chaotic to me?"

"You'll see, I'll explain it as it runs."

"And if we switch, what do you think we'll see?" The professor stepped back from the computer picking up his mug and blowing the mini marshmallows round.

"It could be drastic, like in HG Wells Time Machine; we could end up in a whole new world. Or it could be subtle, like a change of wall colour or something."

The professor laughed. "I can't imagine finding ourselves in a jungle. If we're in a simulation, all the parallels will appear the same, surely? Depending on the cause behind each parallel."

"Well, we're assuming the parallels at this point, Professor - more than the sim I think. And that means we could end up anywhere in the world as we know it, without having any relation to a causality difference."

"What like jumping around the planet or something?"

"Yes, sort of."

"So we could end up on a beach in Maui, for instance?" The professor took a seat in one of the armchairs scattered around and sat back sipping at his drink.

Vladimir smiled. "We could."

"Will there be a variant on when?"

"It's not a time machine Professor, and as far as I've been able to tell there is no way of going back to an old sim; they occur in real time. If there is a storage database then I haven't discovered it yet." Vladimir continued to type commands into the computer, until eventually the scrolling data became more uniform.

"Is that the mainframe you've found there, Vlad?"

"Yes, Professor, I'm in now. When the time comes there'll be a space between the figures."

"And what do we need to do?"

"When it scrolls down to here," Vlad put his finger on one of the screens, "I'll hit enter."

The professor waited but Vladimir didn't continue. "What? That's all?"

"Yep." Vladimir picked up his mug of cocoa and started sipping.

"Sounds a bit simple."

"Trust me Professor, getting to this point was anything BUT simple!"

Vladimir checked his watch and then joined the professor in one of the armchairs. Once they'd finished their drinks, the professor dragged a small table with a chess set across, and said, "You might as well beat me at one last game while we wait."

∞∞∞∞

By the time Vladimir moved his queen into checkmate there were only a few minutes to spare. He smiled at how the professor always put up a good fight on the chess board. Then he moved back to the desk to watch the screen. The professor joined him.

They saw the space appear and begin to work its way down the screen. It felt like an eternity. Vladimir's poised finger began to tremble and he feared he would miss it. But when it arrived it went by the book, although the white flash when he hit enter surprised them both.

Part 3

The professor and Vladimir blinked their eyes repeatedly trying to clear the flash burnt onto their retinas and see behind it. The view had not changed - they were still there, in the Professor's basement, in front of the computer.

The professor looked round while Vladimir sat in closer to the computer screen.

"Did anything change?"

"On the screen it has, Professor."

The professor turned back to the screen and peered at it with Vladimir. It looked strange, chaotic, with far more blank spaces.

"What's happened?"

Vladimir started typing. "I'm not sure … I'm still working it out, but if it is what I think it is, we could be in for a shock."

Vladimir stayed glued to the screen typing at random moments. The professor became irritable. "Well? Come on Vlad, give me something, that flash wasn't just in our imagination."

"Oh no, it definitely wasn't, Professor, it's just … how do I explain it? If I am right we have just accessed the … well like the control panel of the mainframe."

Vladimir glanced at the Professor who was staring at him, but the crease between his eyes indicated that he hadn't fully understood what Vladimir had said.

"It means we've managed to access where the sim is controlled from."

"What, we can now control the sim?" The professor's eyes were wide with trepidation rather than delight.

"Well we can control 'our' sim – our existence within the sim. We can now decide where we want to be – so to speak."

"But the basement is still the same."

"I know, that's puzzled me a little, but I think this is like the constant, the structure, and we can sort of 'download' a different reality outside."

"Outside?" The professor leapt out of his seat. "Well let's not waste any time, let's go and check it out."

It was Vladimir's turn to look concerned, but the professor ignored him and walked to the stairs, taking the steps two at a time. Vladimir rushed after him.

The house was the same but when they looked out of the front room window, life outside wasn't. The snow was gone and sunlight was streaming down. People passing looked different: wearing less, and the style of clothes had changed – they looked more casual and westernised.

"Come on, let's go out and take a look."

When they opened the front door a wall of heat hit them. They both stepped back inside to remove their sweaters. The house looked the same outside as did the surrounding houses, but as they walked down the street other buildings had appeared and more and more people passed them.

In their usual reality, the professor's street was in a quiet residential area, so where were all the people coming from? They found out when they turned the corner at the end of the street and saw all the shops, in particular a string of fast food restaurants.

They stopped and looked wide eyed at each other. It wasn't just the existence of the shops that surprised them but all the displays and sign boards were in English - not Russian. Then they noticed the cars: all new and a wide variety of makes. There was even a Porsche parked outside one of the restaurants – such affluent vehicles would never be parked out in the open in Moscow.

They paused on the side of the street, both unsure what to do. Vladimir turned as though to walk back to the house, but the Professor caught his arm. "Let's go in, let's sample some of the food – I can speak English."

"But we don't have any money."

The professor pulled out his wallet. "Want to bet?" The notes he took out were all green and much narrower than Rubles. Vladimir's mouth fell open. "It seems the sim equips us for all eventualities."

They crossed the street and walked into a restaurant with an ice cream advertisement on the outside. They sat by the window and picked up the menus, trying out some of the words they found on it.

"I'm going to try a 'root beer', see what that's like. What about you, Vlad?"

"I've always been curious about a 'malt'."

When the waitress came over the professor ordered. She didn't seem to bat an eyelid at the heavy Russian accent or at how they were dressed. It was as though she served them every day.

When the drinks arrived a few minutes later they drank them down, enjoying the new flavours. They stared out of the window enthralled by the new world around them - too busy observing to speak.

Then Vladimir spotted it; a black sedan, parked up on the other side of the street, just past the restaurant. He glanced at the professor who followed his gaze.

Two men got out of the car. One of them opened the back door for another man to get out. This man was wearing a blue shiny suit … although the shine was odd, it seemed to fade in and out and ripple across the surface as though playing with the eyes.

Vladimir blinked but it made no difference. And then his eyes moved to the face and he froze - the glass of malt half way to his mouth. The man was looking straight at him.

"He's looking at us, Professor," Vladimir whispered.

"I see that, Vlad."

"What should we do?"

"Nothing, just wait."

The man in the blue suit didn't move. He remained standing there, staring at them through the glass.

"Shouldn't we go out there, Professor?"

"If he wants us, he can come to us."

And as though the man had heard them, he started crossing the street towards them.

Part 4

Their minds saw the man in blue walking, but it appeared like a stream of snap shots as he moved closer. It was fast like a steam train barrelling towards them, arriving before they had the chance to duck to the side. He stopped at the end of the table – the glass window end of the table. It was as though the glass wasn't there - or that he was built into it.

The colour of his suit swirled violently up close. Vladimir felt the malt start to churn in his stomach. He diverted his eyes to the man's face to try and stop it, but looking into his eyes was like looking down a corridor that seemed to go on forever.

Vladimir wrenched his gaze away and looked back into the restaurant. He noticed how nothing else was moving around them. It was like someone had hit pause on the TV. The waitress juggled two coffee cups with one foot off the ground - but there was no wobble or jitter.

"You have activated the Control Panel Wizard."

Vladimir's head spun round. The man had clearly spoken the words, but they seemed to be inside his head rather than out loud.

The professor's eyes met Vladimir's seeking reassurance that he wasn't the only one to have heard it. Vladimir matched his look. Neither of them knew what to do, or understood what it meant.

The man looked at them both.

"I can help you access the reality run you require. Please provide the binary code you were allocated."

Vladimir glanced at the Professor again and then spoke. "We have no code."

A glitch seemed to run through the suit of the man like a line on a screen. He smiled and spoke again. "A binary code is required."

"We were not provided with a binary code."

The man took a slow blink. When his eyes opened again they were black with flashing red pupils.

The professor and Vladimir caught movement behind him as the men from the car came running across.

Then a white flash left the Professor and Vladimir blinking rapidly.

∞∞∞∞

Vladimir kept blinking but his eyes didn't seem to clear. He realised he was lying on his back and assumed he had been thrown back, although he couldn't recall the movement. He heard the professor's voice.

"Vlad? Vlad? Are you there?"

"Yes Professor, I'm here. Are you alright?"

"Yes, but I appear to be lying down."

"Me too."

Vlad moved his hands up to his eyes, continuing to blink, hoping to start seeing something soon. When his hands reached his face he jumped, a cry escaping from his lips.

"What is it Vlad?" The professor started to move himself, and let out a similar cry.

Vladimir's hand pushed at the thing attached to his face, which seemed to be suctioned on. Eventually it moved. When it did, he heard a series of bleeps. He heard the same bleeps come from where the professor was lying. This time when he blinked he could make out shapes and slowly the professor came into view. His eyes also found the source of light: candles on a table between them.

Vladimir took in the room: It was little more than a cell with two cots, and a pile of wires leading to a large machine against the wall. On his body there were tubes and plugs attached and he was horrified to find he even had a catheter. A needle into the main artery in his arm led to a hanging bag.

He swung his legs over the side of the cot. They felt weak and flimsy under him - and so did his mind. When he thought about his home and the University in Russia, it crossed over with thoughts of a different home, a plusher one out in the country – a country that was in the West.

The details of his life in Russia seemed to be fading, like a dream he couldn't quite catch. The name Jonathan came to him; it seemed to match him better. The details of another life belonging to Jonathan flooded his mind.

The professor sat across from him, looking at everything with the same dazed look. Then he said, "Jonathan? Is your name Jonathan?"

"Yes, and you're Augustine, or Ozzy for short? Is that right?"

He nodded, laughing out of disbelief.

"What the hell is this?"

They heard footsteps outside in the corridor and then a clinking sound as some kind of lock was activated. A strange little man put his head round the door and grinned at them.

"Hey guys, how you feeling? Seems you went down the wrong rabbit hole?"

They both looked at him not fully understanding what he was talking about. The guy laughed at them and came into the room. He started removing all the tubes and attachments to their bodies.

"Sorry you're not quite back yet, are you? You tripped the Control Panel Wizard, you weren't meant to do that. Seems you lost this round."

Images of Virtual World Gaming came into Jonathan's mind. "This is a game?"

"Yep. I know you thought you'd just found the answer to life, but sorry to disappoint you, it was all just a game. Why don't you go put your names down, maybe you can try again in another month or so?"

The man pulled out a bag from under their beds and unzipped it.

"Here are your belongings. Take your time. There's no rush." And with that he departed.

Jonathan and Ozzy sat looking at each other, waiting for it all to come back.

The Game

Prologue

The Jester finds himself in a white corridor lined with doors. He knows precisely where he is. It took him an age to work out the nexus points to escape this place and he doesn't want to risk recapture; he has to hurry - just collect them and be gone.

A glance at the corner of the ceiling tells him the little black squares are still there. He doesn't want to be seen on any of them; he has to move fast.

As he had done during his escape, the Jester orientates himself by the numbers painted on the fire extinguishers. There's nothing else to define the different corridors in this labyrinth that makes up the asylum, except by looking in the tiny individual windows on each door. He's not about to do that. He simply needs to reach them without being spotted.

He ducks and jumps his way to the right corridor. He hopes they are still there and haven't been moved. He has no idea how long it has been since he was last here, although he's reassured that with parallel time jumping you always moved forward in time, never back. He counts the doors and selects one, creeping up to it cautiously before peering in. Sure enough there they are, sitting on the white bench provided.

Seeing the inside of the cells again, their blank whiteness, he realises how quickly he's forgotten the isolation: the stillness with everything muffled and sealed with padding. He remembers the claustrophobia that clawed at the edges of his mind and shivers. The girls look so peaceful; the blonde sitting behind the dark-haired one so she can brush her hair. They don't appear anxious or afraid, but then they have each other, and that's a huge comfort in a place like this.

The blonde looks up at the window and pauses when she sees him. She doesn't startle or act surprised, she waits. He smiles, the grin stretching across his parched skin. She doesn't blink. The dark-haired girl joins her, her eyebrows half raised in anticipation.

With the door handles on the outside the Jester is able to go in, but there's also a camera inside. If they come toward the door and vanish, an alarm will be triggered and their escape route blocked. He needs to get them to the nexus point he arrived through as soon as possible, and he needs to persuade them to follow him in a handful of words.

He opens the door a crack and sticks his head in. They don't move, only watch. He whispers, "Girls, if you want to live again you need to come with me quickly – but no questions. Follow my exact movements and I guarantee you safe passage out of here. If you understand and are willing keep brushing her hair."

The blonde girl doesn't hesitate; she starts brushing immediately.

"Good. Now, come on!" he hisses.

They're swift and soundless; their bare feet accommodating this as they rush after the Jester. By the time they turn into the final corridor the alarm bells ring out. They up their pace, the girls hand-in-hand. By the time they pass the extinguisher the Jester noted when he arrived, they can hear heavy footfalls coming after them, but the complexity of the building disguises the direction the sounds are coming from. The girls look around frantically, but the Jester remains focused.

As boot clad feet appear round the corner behind them, everything goes dark, the girls embrace each other as they feel themselves spin.

Chapter 1 – The Net Falls

Her scent reaches him as she joins the group he's standing with. It's exquisite. It makes him stop and stare. On a night like this, when he's busy entertaining all the top-end clients who've turned up to celebrate the fifth birthday of his nightclub, 'Cloud Nine', David isn't expecting to be distracted - but he is.

He watches her glide from person to person introducing herself; smiling, laughing, and talking. He wonders who she is and what she's doing here; he hasn't seen her before and new people are a rarity in his hometown.

David observes her as she makes her way towards him: She's short, but her posture and sense of presence gives her height, making her stand out. Her long blonde hair glimmers in the low light, a piece falls forward over her shoulder as she tilts her head in conversation, framing her face. It sets off her green cat-like eyes, which are striking. He's not the only man watching her. Her kind of beauty is irresistible, and he's riveted.

David's still gazing at her when she turns and walks in his direction. He remains captivated as she strides up to him, extending her hand and saying in a low voice, "Hi, it's David, isn't it? I'm Isabella. I've been looking forward to meeting you, I've heard so much about you and your club." She glances round at the expanse of the nightclub from the third floor balcony they're standing on. "It's a great place you've got here, with an interesting mix of people."

David responds by taking her proffered hand and returning her firm handshake. "Hi Isabella, nice to meet you. Yes, I like it. People come from all over to experience it. A nightclub starting on the nineteenth floor of a skyscraper seems to capture the imagination. It's your first time tonight, isn't it? Can I offer you a tour? Or have you had a look round already?"

"No, I haven't. I'd love you to show me if you have time."

The small smile she gives him, coupled with the way she tilts her head, indicates to David that the attraction's mutual.

"I've got all night."

He offers his arm and she takes it. They walk round the balcony to a small viewing area that looks down on the dance floor below. He talks about the design of the place and how he came up with it. He leans against the chrome railings and points out the DJ's box on the first-floor that's suspended above the dance floor.

"It took a while to work out how to construct that but in the end it worked, thanks to the sound engineers working out the placement of the speakers." David points to various points above and below them on each floor. Small square boxes can be seen on the outside of each balcony corner

Isabella seems to be enjoying the tour. "How many floors are there?"

"There are six in total, each one with its own bar. The sixth floor is the roof terrace and has a second dance floor."

"Wow that sounds spectacular!"

"Come, I'll show you." He offers his arm again and she takes it easily, happy to squeeze into him as they pass people on their way to the elevator. He finds her scent intoxicating.

When they come out onto the roof terrace, it's clear it has been extended on both sides to make room for the dance floor. David leaves Isabella to marvel at it while he goes to the bar for drinks. He watches her walk to the edge and stand on tiptoe to see the view over. The perimeter railing is built on top of a solid half wall for better protection. It's a reach, but she manages it. David admires her agility while he waits for their drinks.

David takes the cocktails over to her and they sip them as they admire the spectacular views the location affords over the dense city. They spend most of the evening there, and David barely notices he's doing most of the talking while Isabella deflects all his questions.

It's only the following morning when he wakes up alone that he starts to think about it. If it wasn't for the tiny note left on the pillow with her number, he might have thought she'd been a figment of his imagination. And even though something about her unsettles him, he puts it down to nerves. It's normal at the beginning of a new relationship to hold back a little. Plus all the non-verbal communication they'd shared had more than made up for it. He's confident it'll improve. How wrong he was.

Chapter 2 - The Chase

David goes to the window and rubs a circle in the filthy pane of glass. This is squalid room in a derelict building, but it gives a good view over the city. The dazzling night lights sprawl beneath him, inviting him in. He hates the rough living he's being forced to endure on this relentless pursuit through parallel times, but give him a city at night and he feels right at home. Having been a nightclub owner in his own time, David comes alive at night, and this twinkling city looks like any other. He's ready to embrace it.

And the Jester is here, David can feel it. His presence is strong - the cackling in his mind is getting louder. He might not have met the Jester in the flesh, but the tentative mental connection they share enables David to track him. David has one last lead on him before the next slip through. He hopes this will be the one that will get him home and bring an end to this loathsome game.

David finds the small, seedy nightclub hidden away in a backstreet. It's called the 'Bull's Tavern' - a rather apt name considering its clientele. He'd heard about it through word of mouth, hanging out in back alleys and on street corners in the rougher parts of the city. It's known as a meeting place for drug dealers, perverts, and other depraved minds - especially those who enjoy a good fight. It seems like the perfect place for the Jester to frequent; his sadistic mind would fit in here perfectly - should he have stumbled upon it, and David really hopes he has.

The entrance is a small door with a red neon sign above it. The stench it emits confirms it's the right place.

Along with the reek of stale beer and bad body odour, there is an underlying scent of blood, further tarnished with the stink of excrement. But instead of going straight in David hangs back, contemplating what's ahead.

Everything has happened so fast since his first slip through. Having witnessed other people going, he'd realised what was happening to him when the bathroom mirror hadn't returned a reflection. It had given him just enough time to dress and grab his wallet before everything had begun to shift and spin and he'd arrived in a motel room in another time.

David is in his third slip through now. The time in each parallel lasts about four days. He has no idea how many slip throughs there will be – whether there is a limit or not. All he knows is he has to catch the Jester if he wants to get home – that's the game.

People in his own time have been playing this game for decades, although no one is ever sure who will be chosen, just that one day you might disappear – vanish in a moment – into another time. He'd watched his own father go. People returned occasionally, but those that did come back didn't like to talk about it much, and when they did they were never sure how many times they had gone through. It was all very vague and traumatising, and now David understands why.

Like a mouse trying to find the cheese in a maze, David is disorientated and exhausted, motivated only by the desire to find a way out and return home. He knows it's possible and the Jester's the key - he just has to catch him.

Cackling fills the back of his mind, low and quiet. Is the Jester listening to his thoughts? It brings the present rushing back to him.

David enters The Bull's Tavern, the men on the door paying him no attention. After the last few days (which feel like months) he knows he looks the part in his dirty, scruffy attire. Inside everything is decked out in red with dim, almost non-existent lighting. The music is loud and harsh, covering the lurid conversations, reducing them to a low background rumble.

David approaches the bar trying to remain casual while scanning the room for any sign of his quarry. Young, worn faces peer back, tales of poverty, desperation and drug abuse etched into them. Others display jeering smiles, enjoying the dark undertone of the place and being among kindred spirits.

David has no idea what the Jester looks like. He imagines someone in his older years, maybe greying, even bald, with a lined, aged face, black eyes and pockmarked skin, probably creased by the high-pitched laughter David hears in his head; a sound that eats into his bones every time he hears it and stays with his every waking moment.

"What'll it be?" a barman yells across the bar at David, his eyes disinterested.

"A beer."

"Beers off, only spirits."

David looks at the rows of bottles unsure of names and tastes.

"What do you suggest?"

The barman rolls his eyes and grabs a bottle off the end of the shelf. He pours a small quantity of brown liquid into a tiny glass and shoves it across the counter. David offers him some money hoping it's enough. The barman snatches it and returns a couple of coins. David picks up the glass and looks at the thick liquid, raising it to his lips for a tentative taste, but the sound of shattering glass interrupts him.

Everybody pauses at the sound; conversation stops, music quiets, all eyes turn to a burly, unshaven man, with arms like balloons, who is holding the jagged edge of a broken bottle to the throat of a small, skinny, greasy-looking man. In the silence the burly man pulls the skinny one up out of his chair, keeping the glass tight up against his throat. Then in one swift movement he swipes it across the man's neck, cutting it clean open, and drops the body on the floor.

No one moves. Everyone holds their breath while the victor throws his head back and lets out a deep, bone-rattling roar. Then all hell breaks loose: tables fly up into the air, glasses smash, fists connect with flesh, and the room fills with the sound of pent up rage and anger.

David decides it's time to leave – fast. But just as he turns to go he's pulled up by the back of the jacket. He braces himself for a punch, but instead someone thrusts a piece of paper into his hand and tells him to "Move!"

With a quick glance he sees it's the barman and he runs for the door. However, in mid-stride his legs stop.

Just above the noise he hears it, high and piercing - the cackle. The Jester is here.

David spins round, searching the entwined mesh of people in front of him. Out of the corner of his eye he sees a cloaked figure on the other side of the room. He can't see the face, just a mouth in an open gape emitting the ear-splitting screech.

David dives into the sprawling mass trying to make his way across. He's kicked and punched as he pushes his way through, and by the time he reaches the other side the Jester is gone.

David stands hunched, gasping for breath, clutching his bruised sides trying to regain his strength. He's unsure what to do, but when a chair goes flying past his head he decides to go back to his original plan and get the hell out. This time he skirts the room and keeps his head down while making his way to the exit.

When he finally reaches the outside world, he slumps down in the alleyway and sticks his head between his legs, trying to process what he's witnessed. His mind reels at the image of such a cold-blooded murder, while trying to recapture the glimpse he had of the Jester. He put his head in his hands, in doing so finding he's still clutching the piece of paper. He opens it with no expectation. It reads one word: "Almost."

It's from the Jester.

David's head swims. Not only has he seen him, he now has written proof of his existence too. He's not an illusion - something David has begun to wonder – he's real.

David puts his head back against the wall and lets out a long sigh, waiting for his body to stop shaking.

What now?

He might not have caught the Jester, but he's accomplished one thing: he's managed to be in the same time and place as him. Can he manage it again?

Chapter 3 – Normality

A few hours later, David is sitting at the bar in the only open establishment he's found in this town. The slip through has gone smoothly. He's getting used to the sensation now; the weightlessness, the dark, with a snippet of time between worlds. With each one he becomes less afraid of what he'll find on the other side.

In this time parallel everything seems to be in decay. Most of the shops are boarded up, some of the buildings crumbling, and the streets are full of debris - there are even unattended fires. People are scarce. Those David has seen appear harried: rushing along, eyes darting around, clothes dishevelled, giving him a wide berth. It makes him uneasy; something isn't right, he feels exposed to a danger he doesn't know about.

But in the restaurant he's found sanctuary. It feels secure, welcoming - a calm in the storm that appears to be going on outside. From the circular bar where he sits he can see the entire room. It's laid out with tables and the bar in the middle. There are small groups of people and individuals dotted all around and at the bar. It's the most people he's seen since he arrived here.

David has yet to get a sense of the Jester. He's been unusually silent since David's arrival. It makes him hard to track.

While David is pondering this, a newly arrived man on his left introduces himself:

"Hi, I'm Rob McCormack. You're a new face in here, aren't you?"

David takes his proffered hand and gives it a firm shake.

"David Sinclair. Yeah, I'm new to this whole town."

"Really? Have you come over from Vernon? I hear things are much worse over there."

David pauses. Rob has a pleasant, relaxed face, with bright inquiring eyes. He's dressed informally in jeans and a checked shirt. David doesn't want to be rude, but he has to be on guard. He knows pretending to be from another town could backfire.

"No. I've been pretty much out of everything for the past ... oh, I don't know, good few months. I've been travelling round. I came back into town to sort of refuel."

"Oh, right." Rob nods.

"Did I miss something? Everything seems to be in a shambles." David knows he's reaching with this question, but he has the impression Rob wants to talk, having opened the conversation and insinuated there's a problem.

"Oh God, yes. You've missed it all!" David's right, Rob's excited to share. "It started about three months ago. They call it a war, but I don't know why, seeing as we don't know who the enemy is."

"What do you mean?" David encourages Rob to continue, relieved the conversation is redirected away from him.

"It's difficult to explain. The government try to cover it up as much as possible, although it's hard to miss what's going on with so many people disappearing. The work force has been decimated - that's why everything's in such a state. So far there doesn't seem to be a shortage of food, but clothes, electronics, stuff like that, they're getting hard to come by."

"I don't understand, why?"

"As I said before, no work force. There's no delivery of these goods coming in from other states. Oh it's all screwed up!"

"What do you mean by people disappearing? Do they run off, what?"

A strange expression comes over Rob's face: a mixture of fear and resignation. David feels a chill creep up his spine as he recognises it.

"No, they just disappear ... sort of vanish. One minute they're standing there in front of you, then the next ... their image kind of ... wobbles, like it's coming from a film projector or something, then it fades out and they're gone."

The haunted look in Rob's eyes reminds David of his own after he witnessed his father going. It further increased when his best friend, John, went too, despite not having seen him physically go. David remains silent, the memories keeping him tongue tied. Rob has also stopped speaking, stalled by the memory. They both sip their drinks.

"So," Rob almost shouts, bringing his fist down on the bar, jolting David back to reality. "Where are you staying?"

"I don't know yet. I'll probably find a motel somewhere."

"I don't think you'll have much luck, they're all closed. With people disappearing in their rooms they don't get payment. They can't afford to stay open."

"I'll work something out. Do you want a drink?" David's used to making do since slipping through. He knows he'll be able to find a derelict or empty building to bunk down in.

"If you're sure, I'll have another one of these." Rob tips his glass at the barman who nods.

"So Rob, how long have these disappearances been going on?" David's curious if this is the same thing that's happening in his own time – it sounds like it. Although everyone in his time knows it can happen, they're even taught about it in school; and it's random and infrequent not hundreds of people going every day. Did Rob know about the Jester? Could Rob be a part of one of the Jester's games? He wouldn't put anything past him.

"Around three months or so, I think. It could be longer, but with the sheer numbers of people vanishing things are crumbling fast."

"And you believe it's some kind of war?"

"Well that's vague. Media has crashed too, no reporting, few broadcasts about anything. What's left of the government is trying to quell the panic and keep order – although it's not working as you can see by the state of things outside. Randall here has kept this place going by keeping it locked tight at night and having an armoury of sorts behind his counter." Randall smiles and lifts up a large gun he has hidden to support Rob's point. "But we don't know who's causing the disappearances, or why people are going: maybe some kind of science experiment, teleportation or something. I have no idea. It's all so bizarre."

David nods as Rob downs his new drink. "Any idea where they go?"

"Not a clue."

"And they don't come back?"

"Not that I've seen. Could be alien abductions for all I know." Rob chuckles but there's an edge to it as though he knows it might not be a joke. "Have you really not seen anything like this while you've been out travelling?"

David shakes his head. "I've been camping out rough in woods and forests, sort of getting back to nature, survival type stuff." David hopes this also explains his current appearance. "I haven't been in many towns or around people for a while."

Rob tips his glass at Randall and another round of drinks is distributed. David tries to keep up, but can already feel the effects of the drinks he's had so far. It's been a long time since he's had alcohol – or at least it feels like a long time. Rob continues.

"All I know is that if it keeps on like this I'm going to wish I could disappear too. It's horrible seeing it all crumble like this."

"I can imagine." David thinks of his own time and the heart break from the disappearances they had – but they also had hope that people might return as some of them did. They had set time limits as nobody had ever returned after two months, and it helped to reduce the anxiety of waiting and to give closure. There seemed no rational to it in this time. "Do you live nearby?"

"Over the back, behind here." Rob waves his arm in a vague direction behind the restaurant. "It's a nice little apartment. Used to be a nice neighbourhood before all this. Now I have to barricade myself in when I'm home and leave it looking like a shithole on the outside to keep the looters out."

"Looters?"

"Yeah, there's always someone ready to take advantage when things go awry. Steal the clothes off your back some of them." Rob swallows his drink in one gulp again as David struggles to get through half of his. "Another one, David?"

"Not for me, but please have another on me."

"I can't do that to you. You don't even know where you're going to rest your head tonight."

"I'll be fine." David's head's spinning and he has to concentrate to form words.

Rob gives David a side glance. "You're welcome to come and crash at mine if you like." He doesn't sound comfortable making the offer and David isn't sure about accepting it.

"No, I don't want to impose. Plus you only met me half an hour ago."

"Yeah, maybe. But you seem like a nice enough guy - open, sociable, honest. I haven't met many like that for some time; everyone's so shady and secretive these days.

To be honest, I'd be glad of the company." He sounds more confident as he speaks.

"It's okay, Rob. I'm confident I'll find somewhere."

Rob half laughs. "I'm not. I really don't think you will, Dave – can I call you that?" David nods - he likes the familiarity of it. It's been a long time since he's had a normal conversation with anyone. "Look, I can only offer you my sofa, but you're welcome to stay as long as you need. Having someone around to chat to would make a nice change."

He seems determined, and David's too drunk to put up any resistance.

"OK, as long as you're sure; that'd be great."

Rob smiles at him and claps him on the shoulder.

"Good. Right, now that's sorted lets have another round."

They continue to make small talk as they drink, sharing backgrounds, interests, finding common ground. David orders something to eat to soak up the drink, and when he finishes the barman puts a bill in front of him. It reads '12.87'. David is unsure if the notes he has are valid here. He glances at Randall and mumbles, "I'm not sure if these are worth anything anymore ..." and pushes a couple of tens across the bar.

The barman's eyes light up. He picks them up gently as though they might break, his mouth dropping open. Rob stops drinking beside him and gives a low whistle. David glances at him, unsure if it's good or bad.

"What?"

"Good God, Dave, where the hell did you get your hands on all that?" Rob's staring at the rest of the notes he has in his hand.

"What do you mean?"

"What do I mean?! Christ! That stuff's like gold dust. It's the old money, double the value of the new stuff they issued a couple of months ago. You're lucky if you can get your hands on just one of those notes, let alone that many!"

David stares at the fan of money in his hands.

Rob takes a sharp look over each shoulder. "I'd watch where you flash that if I was you, you'll end up getting mugged."

"Don't worry I'll keep it safe." David stuffs it into the inside pocket of his jacket.

Randall is still rooted to the spot, his eyes glued to the two notes in his hands. David decides to be generous - apparently he can afford to be.

"It's alright, keep the change."

The comment seems to break the barman's trance: delight blossoms on his face. "Thank you, thank you so much." He rushes to the cash drawer and swiftly puts them in, making furtive glances around him as he does so. David smiles.

"You looked bushed Dave, I think we should make tracks." Rob takes the last swig of his drink and David nods in agreement. The alcohol has relaxed him and the tensions of survival and being on high alert have gone; he's exhausted.

Chapter 4 - Connections

David lies back on Rob's sofa, the softest place he's slept in a long time. He considers how quickly he feels at home here, in this luxurious one bedroom flat, and how relaxed he is in Rob's company after only a few hours of knowing him.

After they left the restaurant, Rob had led David through a labyrinth of alleyways behind it to what looked like the back of an abandoned, boarded up building. They'd gone up some metal stairs to a back door and Rob had undone several complicated locks to let them into the kitchen. But before turning on the lights Rob had relocked the door and made sure it was secure - he wasn't taking any risks.

Once the lights were on, a spotless deluxe kitchen was revealed. David had to squint against the gleaming white cabinets and tiles; he hadn't seen anything that clean in a while. And when Rob takes him round the rest of the flat all he says is 'wow'. Rob then sets David up with bedding for the night and shows him where the bathroom is, telling him all the facilities are at his disposal. They don't chat much, both tired and a little drunk. Rob says goodnight and goes off to bed.

All the windows are boarded up and there's no natural light, but the opulence and plush furnishings are still apparent even in the soft lighting. It reminds David of his own flat back in his own time, and the soft fabrics resemble those used in his nightclub. It brings on a wave of homesickness. But there's no awkwardness or tension about David being here – it feels like they're old friends.

It's strange. And it brings back memories of his best friend John.

John slipped through a couple of months before David and David felt his loss keenly. Their mothers had been best friends so they'd grown up together, and being only children they'd considered themselves brothers. They'd seen each other almost every day.

As David pulls up the quilt, he recalls moments of their life together. One in particular stands out: John's father's funeral.

The service had taken place at the graveside and they had all returned to the house - or so David had thought until he noticed John wasn't with him. He'd found him at the foot of his father's freshly covered grave, hands clasped, tears rolling down his face, oblivious to the outside world. John's whole body had jerked when David had put a hand on his shoulder.

"Hey John. Come on back to the house. Your mum needs you." He'd stood patiently at John's side, waiting for him to collect himself.

John's dad hadn't been an old man when he'd died; cancer had cut him down in his prime. David knew that John had expected his father to beat it - even convinced himself that he would, but now he was standing looking at his gravestone.

"I can't believe he's gone David, you know?" David had remained silent, letting John talk. "I thought he'd be able to fight it, rid himself of it. I mean he was my DAD, David, he could do anything! When mum first told me I thought she was being melodramatic; I thought there was bound to be something that would work, that would stop it, that dad could take, you know, to break it down. But she was right, there wasn't. And now he's gone." John had paused, trying to control his emotions, but he had started sobbing instead. David had put his arm round John and pulled him in while he spat out the rest of his feelings:

"And all I could do was watch him go, just fade away, totally fucking helpless! Totally fucking useless!"

The tears had come thick and fast, until he could no longer speak. David had pulled out a handkerchief and handed it to him without speaking, and they'd stayed that way for some time, staring at the wreaths, waiting for John's tears to subside. Then they'd walked back to the house together.

This memory sparks another, one of David's own father going, just a couple of years later - although not to the grave.

David's father had been pulled into the parallel universes at the Jester's bidding, like his son. David remembers the garbled phone call he'd made to John and John rushing over. John had let himself in with the spare key and found David sitting in the lounge, dumbstruck, with tears streaming down his face. John had sat down next to him and put his hand on David's shoulder. David had registered his presence with a slight turn of the head as he told him what had happened.

"He was right here, John, right here, talking to me." David had pointed to the spot with a shaky hand. "Mum was sitting there," he'd pointed at the armchair by the door, "and his image went all funny - sort of opaque. We knew before he did. You should've seen his face, John, when he realised what was happening - the panic! Then mum started screaming." David had sniffed back more tears. "He won't be back, John, I just know it. He won't be back."

"Oh come on Dave, you don't know that. Your uncle came back." John had tried to console him.

David had shaken his head - he'd been resolute. "He won't, I can feel it."

John had refused to accept his statement. "You mustn't think like that, David. There's always hope."

David sighs at the memory and wonders as he drifts off to sleep whether John still believes in that hope now that he, himself is lost out here in the myriad of time parallels too. Did he still hope to return? Did he even have a chance?

***

David walks forward, clouds of mist streaming past him. He can see only grey, until a shape starts to form in the distance. As he draws closer he can make out something tall. It's black at first, but as it comes into focus he can see the top is lighter. He's only a few paces away when he realises it's the Jester with his back to him.

David moves round until he's standing in front of him. But it isn't the Jester, it's Isabella. She's standing quite still, just looking at him. She's beautiful. He can feel his desire rising.

He tries to lift his arms to touch her, but nothing happens; the more he tries the more upset he becomes. He tries to call out her name, but he can't make a sound.

A smile appears on her face. It broadens, exposing her teeth - encrusted yellow teeth, with green, putrid gums. They don't belong to her, they belong to the Jester. Isabella's head tilts back, her mouth opens wide, letting loose a soundless laugh. David tries to run, to get away from the repulsive sight, but he can't. He runs on the spot like he's on a treadmill. The Jester's playing his sick mind games again.

***

David sits bolt upright on the sofa, sweat running down his face and body. The Jester's here.

He sits round on the sofa, pulling the quilt off the floor where he's kicked it in his haste to try and get away from the man in his dreams. He gathers it round his shoulders and puts his head in his hands, calming his breathing, waiting for his heart to stop racing.

He's suspected the two of them were connected somehow, but this is the first time he's had confirmation.

His uncle's words, 'You'll soon realise you were chosen to go' come into his mind, words that since slipping through have haunted him almost as much as the Jester's cackle.

David's uncle had returned a broken man after his time with the Jester. As a young teenager, after he'd understood the possibility of slipping through himself, David had become fascinated by people going and the stories of those that had returned. When he'd found out he had a family member who'd returned he'd tried to glean as much information as possible. But his uncle had become withdrawn - even anxious, struggling to come to terms with what he'd been through. Those words had been one of the few things he'd said before he'd taken his own life a year later. They hadn't made much sense to David at the time, but once John had gone, he started to piece it together. And now David himself had gone their meaning had begun to unfurl.

David recalls a framed photograph his uncle used to keep on the mantelpiece. His uncle would pick it up and gaze at it when David would ask him about his time away. It was a photograph of a woman his uncle had been in relationship with before he'd slipped through. David wishes he could take a look at it now. He's confident he'd see a familiar face.

But if it was Isabella in the photo – or Annie – how did his father get chosen? David believed his parents had always been devoted to each other, but could his father have had an affair? Had he betrayed his mother? Or did David have it wrong? Maybe it didn't have to be a romantic relationship. Maybe his father had met one of them through his work or socially. David doesn't know – all he knows is that if the Jester is teasing him with Isabella it means there's a connection. How else would the Jester know about her?

Isabella's behaviour had always been odd, even on the night he'd met her. She'd been remote and hard to pin down, avoiding any conversation about her past and refusing to commit emotionally to their relationship. He had wanted more than an affair but she had resisted, and he'd relented not wanting to risk losing what they had. He'd been besotted with her from their first night together, and he'd seen only what he had wanted to see. And when John had started dating her best friend, Annie, it had become easier; they had spent time together as a foursome, which meant more time with Isabella. David hadn't liked how secretive she'd been and all the whispered conversations she'd had with Annie, but the pay off of being in her company had been worth it.

Then Annie had disappeared a few weeks before John had slipped through and Isabella a few weeks before David had gone, and his suspicions had started to grow.

People had said the girls had slipped through too, but David didn't believe it. The one thing that had come through in all his research about slipping through was it was the men that went; barely a handful of women had gone and reports had been questionable – their spouse's accounts considered dubious by law enforcement. And his suspicions had been fuelled further when he found all their belongings gone too. Nobody took their stuff with them when they slipped through, they didn't have time. He'd looked into their background to track down relatives and come up empty; there'd been no trace of them. It was like they had never existed.

He knew it was why he hadn't been surprised the morning he'd felt himself going - he'd expected it; he'd been counting the days since Isabella had left, and the morning he went was exactly the same number of days John had gone after Annie's departure.

And now he has confirmation. It might not be tangible; it might just be a dream to some, but David knows better - the Jester doesn't put anything into your mind unless it's part of the game.

There's a light knock at the lounge door and Rob's head appears. "Ah good, you're up. Fancy some breakfast?"

Chapter 5 – Recruitment

Isabella runs as hard as she can, but the soft sand steals her footfalls and slows her progress. When she hits the deck of the jetty she speeds up, flinging herself over the rail at the end, gasping for air.

While she hangs there, she looks down into the depths of the lake, letting her eyes trace the hundreds of thrombolites sitting at the bottom. They've been down there since the beginning of time, believed to be responsible for oxygenating the earth. They remind her of how trivial she really is, her tiny life span insignificant against these living rocks, reducing her to nothing but a blip in the whole space-time continuum. No matter how screwy things get you can't mess with that fact, it grounds you – and things have got screwy – real screwy!

They thought they'd done the right thing letting the Jester break them out of the asylum, but they were wrong. When they'd come into contact with him on the inside, when he'd been an inmate, they'd thought him a quirky but harmless man. They'd laugh along with everyone at the tricks he'd pull: making the orderlies trolleys vanish, materialising food they hadn't seen in years; they hadn't questioned it, just enjoyed it. So when he'd offered them their freedom they hadn't hesitated, knowing that if anyone could get them out, he could, not thinking about the consequences - or the pay back.

Now Annie has disappeared and Isabella has no idea how to find her. She keeps having dizzy spells and finding herself in different times and strange locations making it hard to keep up with him. He's always one step ahead of her, leading her on with his laughter, but she knows that without him she'll never see her sister again.

Isabella brings herself up to standing and looks out over the watery vista. She spots something floating on the surface, its bright colour giving it away against the landscape. It looks like some kind of flower but as more objects appear she isn't so sure. Then hundreds come into view, cresting the ripples of the lake, sporting an array of colours: orange, red, pink, yellow, purple, green, blue, turquoise, and some with patterns.

Isabella bends down under the railings, leaning out over the edge of the jetty to grab one as they drift past. When she scoops one up she sees it's a tiny origami bird, perfectly folded, with a long neck. They're his, she's sure of it. He always has something in his hands, always fiddling; his restless nature demanding it. Her heart rate quickens and her stomach starts to churn. She gathers up more, bringing them out of the water, inspecting each one, even unfolding a couple in case they hold a message of some kind. Then she hears his cackle in her head and her eyes flick up. She scans the shore line, but no one is there.

Isabella stands up, putting a handful of the paper birds in her pocket without thinking. She continues to examine the area for any sign of him as she makes her way off the jetty. Once she reaches the sand his cackle grows louder and she sets off at a run in the direction she thinks it is coming from.

She doesn't get far before everything wobbles and she finds herself running on tarmac down an empty street at night. But she doesn't slow down - it could be dangerous.

Isabella runs through the city with a growing awareness that there aren't any people around at all: the streets are deserted. She reduces her sprint to a jog. As she approaches the end of the street, a building catches her eye: it could be how the old theatre is lit or how the show title glares out at her, but his cackle in her mind confirms that she's reached her destination.

She stops to catch her breath in the middle of the street and reads the sign: 'The Jester presents' is emblazoned in big red letters across the front, and underneath in much smaller gold italics are the words: 'Isabella gets her guy'.

Isabella takes tentative steps up to the big wooden front doors and pushes on one of them. It swings open. Inside, the front-of-house foyer is fully lit. Its ornate red and gold décor gives her the feeling she's stepped back in time. No-one's there, just black arrow signs pointing the way. She walks through, taking the red carpeted stairs up to the internal wooden doors. She pushes on the long brass handles, entering the theatre's auditorium on the ground floor.

It's empty inside. The red velour seating faces a low-lit, red velvet curtain, edged in gold, which hides the stage behind it. A sign standing to one side of the curtain says, 'Take a seat'. Isabella glances round taking in the three decorative tiered balconies with their gold edging, and makes her way along one of the middle rows of seating until she reaches the centre and sits down.

As soon as she does, music starts and the lights change. The curtain rises and there he is standing with his arms open as though ready to receive a room full of people: The Jester. He has on what looks like a black magician's suit, but there is no top hat covering his almost bald head; its white wisps of hair and encroaching liver spots are on full display under the stark spotlight, his pale aged face displaying his yellow-toothed grin and tiny black specks for eyes.

"Ladies and gentlemen," he announces to the theatre at large, as though there are other people present. "Tonight we have a special treat. Isabella will come and join me up here on stage."

There is applause and Isabella whips her head round looking for the other patrons, but there are none to be found.

The Jester looks straight at her and beckons her to join him. She stands up and moves to the central aisle, walking down to the stage. There she finds steps up to it and as she climbs the Jester steps forward to take her hand. His fingers are cold and dry, almost papery to the touch, and Isabella resists the urge to pull hers back once she's up on the stage with him.

"Isabella, it's so nice to see you out of your padded cell."

Isabella remains silent, knowing the disdain she feels is visible on her face. He might consider himself her saviour but this endless chase is making her long for the peace and solitude of the asylum.

"Are you ready for me to reveal what I have in mind for you? What it is I want from you in return for your freedom?"

His tiny black eyes regard Isabella with an intensity she recoils from. She nods, unable to vocalise an answer, wrapped as it is in fear and trepidation at what the price for her release might be.

"I need you to be my recruitment officer." Isabella frowns as the Jester continues. "There is a wealth of strong, handsome young men I want as players for my game, and you, my dear, have the wiles to unearth them and reveal their vulnerabilities to me."

Isabella baulks. "What? You want me to prostitute myself for you and your games?" She snatches her hand away, pleased to finally be able to do so. "I'm not about to become anyone's sex slave. I'd rather be returned to my cell – at least there I'm safe. And where's my sister, Annie? What have you done with her?"

She expects the Jester to placate her, to sooth her and talk her into whatever he wanted, but he doesn't.

"For a cell bunny that hasn't seen daylight for many years, you're behaving like a spoilt brat, aren't you?" He turns grinning at the imaginary audience. Isabella hears their laughter. "And your sister's doing just fine, enjoying her own little journey. You'll get to be together soon - if you play well."

Isabella jerks at his harsh tones. "Spoilt? Being thrown into chaos: jumping from place to place, time to time, wondering what's going on, you call that spoilt?" She spits the last words at him and he wipes his eyes in a dramatic effect, dusting down his coat in exaggerated movements, playing to the invisible crowd before he speaks again.

"My dear, I had to test you, see your strengths and abilities to know that you were right for the team. As for sex that's your choice. I simply need you to identify the strong characters within the given societies; the ones you think will play my games the best."

"And how will I get to these 'societies'?" Isabella attempts to cover her feelings of foreboding with an indignant tone.

"Oh don't worry about that, I'll show you a neat little trick I came across. Come." He leads her across the stage to a small white cross taped onto the black floor. "See this?"

She nods.

"When you step on it you will find yourself in another place. These little 'doorways' as I like to call them, can be found all over the place. I'll lead you to them each time you need to 'move on'."

Isabella looks at the spot, then at the Jester. She has no reason to doubt him as she's already passed through many in her pursuit.

He puts his palm out. "Shall we?"

"What? Now?"

"No time like the present." And then he laughs, along with the audience, the irony of his statement amusing them.

His high-pitched cackle pierces Isabella's ears as she puts her hand in his. Then he pulls her forward onto the cross and everything around her swirls into blackness.

Chapter 6 - Appearance

"So if you're still up for clubbing tonight, it might be an idea to get you some new clothes." Rob points a buttered knife at David's dirty t-shirt. David looks down at himself and knows Rob is right. Caring about his appearance is a luxury slipping through doesn't afford; priorities such as finding food, shelter and the Jester take precedence. "I know a place that's still open and has some okay stuff. We'll pop by there in a bit."

Rob has provided a luxurious breakfast - although any food for breakfast is a luxury for David at the moment. He has tried to pace himself and not gorge too much, but he has to try every topping and every type of bread on offer. Rob doesn't seem fazed by it, and keeps a continuous supply of hot toast coming.

When David mentions he used to be a nightclub owner, Rob gets excited and insists that they try out the one he frequents. David is surprised it's still running, but Rob says it's thriving with everywhere else shutting down. David thinks it can't do any harm to have a day off; he's confident he'll be here for at least four days, which seems to be the current duration between each slip through. And with no lead on the Jester yet, it can't hurt to check out the area.

"I'm not sure I can afford to be a snazzy dresser."

"I am - that stash you've got will go a long way."

David pulls a face as he takes another slice of toast. "I don't want to blow it all at once."

"Trust me, you won't be able to." Rob chuckles.

"So how long have you been going to this club?"

"Years! But it's changed a bit, and certainly recently. No one trusts anyone anymore and it can get a bit rough. I've been a couple of times on my own but it's not much fun. It'll be good to have some company."

"A wing man!"

Rob laughs. "Yeah something like that. People don't interact like they used to; everyone's suspicious of everyone else. It's crazy."

"Insecurity brings out the worst in people."

"It sure does."

"Do you think there'll be an end to it?"

"Maybe, I don't know. Maybe once everyone has gone."

"Do you think it'll come to that?"

"I really don't know. If I had a clue what was really going on I might be able to speculate. But that's the thing, nobody does and it makes everyone edgy."

David chews on his toast and nods. He thinks about how he has some answers, although he knows those answers won't help Rob – if anything they'll make it more complicated. He watches Rob start to put away the breakfast things and decides that now isn't a good time. He also likes the idea of spending the evening in the company of someone - it feels like it's been a long time. Revealing to Rob that he's from another time and that this whole thing is a game would ruin that. Plus he has no idea where he'd begin. He'll sit on it for now. Meantime, they have shopping to do.

David finds it peculiar going clothes shopping – a relaxed, every day event, in another time parallel. The feeling is heightened by his focus shifting from chasing a dark, elusive man who holds the answers to his predicament to looking at clothes and what might look good for a night out. On the one hand it feels wrong and like he shouldn't be wasting his time, but on the other it feels good: normal and calming.

The shop Rob suggests is big and spacious and has a large range of clothes. There are freestanding circular clothes racks scattered throughout, and they both take their time going through them. Besides Rob, who's standing at the rack next to David, the only other person in the shop is an assistant who's busy arranging shelves at the back.

David has a pair of navy trousers over one arm, ready for purchase, and is trying to find a shirt to match them. He moves over to the rack Rob's looking through when another man walks in.

David glances at him and notes the long heavy coat and wide-brimmed hat. Rob glances at him too and raises an eyebrow at David indicating it isn't just him that thinks the man looks out of place.

The man moves round the shop fondling all the shirts down one side, and studies a few as though searching for one in particular. He eventually works his way round to the rack David and Rob are standing at. The assistant pays him no attention, but Rob is watching him, causing David to do the same.

David can only see the bottom half of the man's face under his hat. He has a long chin with a few days stubble on it. He appears dishevelled as though he'd been in the same clothes for several days, which isn't exceptional here, but David is transfixed as though compelled to watch his every move.

The man starts to finger the clothes next to David, touching each item and looking hard at the fabric, the brim of his hat almost touching the rack. Then he speaks: "Enjoying the little lapse, are we?"

David stiffens, his eyes moving from the man's fingers to his face. He expects to see the Jester but instead finds a rugged, middle-aged man. This is not the man he glimpsed in the Bull's Tavern or in his dreams. The man smiles.

"Don't look so surprised, David, you knew I was here. Isabella's rather beautiful, isn't she? I did enjoy being in her."

David opens his mouth to speak but he's at a loss for words.

"Oh come now, so tense? That won't benefit you. You have to be loose and flexible if you want to catch me."

This breaks David's paralysis; he grabs the man's forearm, but the man only smiles wider and shakes his head.

"No, no, no. As I am, David, as I am." His eyes start to change. "The man I am currently occupying isn't much good to you."

David loosens his grip and the man steps back, his face beginning to change. David glances at Rob whose shocked expression tells him he's not the only one witnessing this transformation.

The eyes on the man's face go dark and the skin starts to break up; clumps of pink flesh roll up and drop to the floor revealing the grey taut skin beneath. He opens his mouth exposing rotting teeth and starts to cackle, the laughter growing louder as he walks backwards out of the shop.

David and Rob remain rooted to the spot throughout, until the Jester passes through the doorway. When their paralysis breaks and David realises what he has to do: now the Jester is himself, he has to catch him.

He drops the clothes he's holding and runs. The Jester is out of sight by the time he reaches the door, but he catches a flash of his coat-tails as he disappears down an alleyway on the left. David gives chase, hearing Rob behind him as they both skid round the corner, sprinting hard until it dawns on them he's no longer in sight.

David can hear his cackle rising to its screaming crescendo.

"Can you hear it?" he yells at Rob.

"Hear what?"

"His laughter." David's pace slows.

"I can't hear a thing." Rob comes to a stop, bending over to catch his breath. "Who is he?"

David stops too. "Just a ghost from the past." The cackle starts to fade.

"What? That's a pretty lively ghost if you ask me."

David turns round and starts walking back up the alley.

"Where are you going?" Rob calls after him.

"To buy those clothes."

Rob pauses for a moment, blinking, and then follows.

Chapter 7 – Catalyst

Rob and David dance a lot on their night out. The dance floor is packed and the tunes keep on coming. David is surprised by how many he knows – time parallels are strange. He enjoys being able to get lost in the music and not think about where he is for a moment - or who he is chasing.

Despite having a strong fitness regime in his own reality, David can't keep up with Rob. His stamina has been eroded by trying to keep his wits about him and orientate himself every few days, let alone the lack of decent or regular meals. When it's his turn to buy another round of drinks, he uses it as an excuse to take a break.

The club is small: it comprises a large room on the ground floor, dominated by a wooden dance floor in its centre. A bar runs along the wall at the back and there's a raised walkway that leads from it on both sides and encircles the room so people can move around with their drinks without crossing the dance floor. Booth seating is provided against the walls inside the walkway. Rob managed to grab a free one when they first arrived. David sits down in it and observes the room. His eyes sweep across the counter of the bar and the backs of two women catch his eye: one with long dark hair, the other with long blonde hair. Rob comes over and joins him.

"What are you looking at?" He tries to follow David's gaze.

"Those two over there." David nods his head towards the women. "One dark, one blonde. Isn't it time we did some asking?"

"Let me catch my breath first. What do their faces look like? I don't think I've seen them in here before."

And as though on cue, the blonde turns round and faces them.

The hair on the back of David's neck bristles. He stares at the face unable to accept what he is seeing: Isabella is looking straight back at him.

"Looks like she's already interested, David." Rob nudges him and smiles, but David's expression makes him falter. "Hey Dave, are you alright man?"

David knows she's recognised him by how intently she's staring. He waits, wondering what she's going to do. The girl next to her turns to see what her friend is looking at, and freezes upon seeing him. David finds himself blinking unbelievingly at Annie.

They appear to be waiting for him to do something - he doesn't.

Rob's getting a little worried. "Dave? Dave, who is she? Do you know her?"

David doesn't take his eyes off them. "Yes."

Isabella has started to move, collecting herself together. Annie follows suit.

"There's no time to explain now, I've got to get hold of her." He stands up and puts his glass down. "She's got the answers I need, I'm sure of it."

Rob opens his mouth to say something, but David doesn't give him time; he moves past him and rushes towards the bar.

When he sees them move towards the exit he picks up speed, pushing people aside to get through. By the time Isabella and Annie reach the exit door, David is only a couple of steps behind them, and before the door bounces back he slides through it, just in time to see them rushing away up the alleyway behind the club. They don't look back.

David takes the opportunity to move up behind them in a few silent strides, although just as he makes a grab for

Isabella's arm Annie spots him and lets out a scream, causing them both to start running. But David snags Isabella's sleeve before they take off and manages to pull her back, swinging her round to face him.

"Don't rush off, Isabella, we need to talk."

"Leave me alone David." She wriggles in his grip.

"How did you get here? And who are you really, Isabella? He sent you, didn't he? Didn't he?" David backs her up to the wall of the alleyway so she can't get away.

"Leave her alone!" Annie's behind him, thumping him on the back. He pushes back against her and she loses her footing, sitting down hard on the ground.

"I'm not answering any of your questions, David, unless you let me go!" Isabella wrenches her arm free and David stands waiting.

"Go on then, answer them."

Isabella rubs her arms. "I don't know what you want me to say."

David lets out an exasperated laugh. "What's your connection to him?"

"I don't know what you're talking about." She refuses to make eye contact and keeps trying to look round at Annie. David takes her arm again to get her attention, his anger rising – she's messing with him.

"You know exactly what I'm talking about, Isabella. He sent you. You picked me - you came to my nightclub and sought me out for him, didn't you? And Annie too, she chose John - she took John! Or do you just identify them for him? Huh?" Isabella keeps her eyes on the ground as she tries to free her arm. "Look at me Isabella! Tell me why you're doing this."

"I'm not doing anything - you are! Let me go!"

"I will not!" Rage courses through him as he thinks about all he has been through. He takes her by the shoulders and pushes her hard up against the wall, the thud audible, but he doesn't feel sorry about it, not while she's playing the Jester's games. "Tell me where he is, right now! And John, what have the two of you done with him?"

Isabella gives him a reproachful look as she wipes the back of her hand across her mouth and then spits in his face. Out of shock and rage David lifts his hand to strike her but the loud slam of the exit door stops him.

It's Rob. He's standing at the door observing David about to hit a woman, his expression a mixture of confusion and concern. He clearly doesn't like what he's seeing. David lowers his arm, humility and shame quenching his anger.

"You need to tell me how I can get out of here, Isabella, and where I can find him. Don't pretend you don't know. You owe me that much at least, after all you've put me through."

Isabella stops studying her feet and looks at him, this time with regret in her eyes. "I'm sorry David, but I had to."

"Had to?"

"Yes. You don't understand, he saved us, we owe him."

"Are you his prisoners, Isabella? You and Annie? Is he forcing you to do this?"

"You don't get it. We have a gift so they locked us up. He gave us our freedom."

"At a price ..."

"Yes at a price, David." Isabella glares at him. "Everything comes at a price, even freedom."

"Maybe I can help you? Maybe we can help each other?" David hates hearing himself plead.

The anger in Isabella's eyes fades. "I have to go now. I'm sorry."

She moves to one side, sliding away from David along the wall, waiting for him to grab her again. He doesn't. The desire to fight her has gone. Annie, who's back on her feet, takes Isabella's outstretched hand.

"Can you at least tell me where John is? Annie? You must know where he is, seeing as you sent him there."

Annie doesn't answer; she only gives him a meek look before turning away. They start walking, looking over their shoulders every couple of seconds to make sure he isn't creeping up behind them. David can't believe he's letting them go.

"Wait." He runs to catch up with them, but when he reaches out a hand to Isabella's shoulder, it goes straight through her. He looks at his hand in amazement.

The girls stop walking and turn slowly, their smiles sad, their eyes glass-like. Their teeth begin to change. David watches them turn from white, to yellow, to brown and then a pitted grey, their gums corroding along with them, ending in a rancid green that almost glows in the night light.

Then they start to laugh, but like their smiles this disintegrates too. In between the bursts of their laughter David can hear the Jester's breaking through, until only that is left. The image of the girls thins and wafts in the night breeze until it vanishes all together. A figure appears at the top of the alleyway. It's the Jester.

David is unsure what to do. Should he give chase? He gave chase earlier and it got him nowhere. But tonight the figure isn't moving. Is he waiting for David? The cackle stops.

Rob joins David. He whispers, "Is that the guy from the shop?" David nods.

David looks at Rob while contemplating his next move. If giving chase is useless maybe it's his turn to play with the Jester a little, tease him for a change and see how he likes it. A smile dances on David's lips at the thought. It's time to turn the tables.

Rob gives him a puzzled look, but David remains silent, staring deep into Rob's eyes hoping he'll understand and pick up his intention. David hears movement. The Jester has turned his back on them - but is still there.

David can feel the Jester probing around in his head trying to work out what he's planning. David clears his mind, thinking only of the grasslands and landscape from home – the wide-open spaces. The Jester doesn't like it. He spins back, facing them once more, and just for a second David glimpses a look of annoyance on his face.

That's when David goes, running as fast as he can, determined to get him this time, but the figure leaps into action just a fraction behind, disappearing round a corner just as David reaches it. David carries on running, but falters to a stop when he realises the Jester has gone again.

Rob appears at his side, breathing hard. "Wh ... where's he gone?"

David lifts his hands up with a shrug. "You tell me."

"Oh God, not again!"

With these kinds of tricks David doesn't stand a chance.

Chapter 8 – Catch me if you can

When they get back to Rob's flat, David knows it's explanation time.

Rob knows David isn't from here, but he's stunned when he finds out how literally he means it – not just another place, but another place in time. He's fascinated by David's story and how he has been slipping through times chasing this elusive man. He wonders out loud who the Jester is and why he's doing this and David tells him everything he knows – including his uncle's words and his suspicions about Isabella and Annie, which have now been confirmed and yet pose more questions: What is this gift she referred to? Who locked them up and why? Can they do what he does? How did the Jester know about them, let alone free them? Are they just pawns in his game like David, or is there some other connection? They spend hours discussing all the possibilities. But when it comes to the dilemma about how to catch the Jester, Rob wants in.

"It's not like there's anything else for me here. As you've seen it's all falling apart. I'm just going through the motions, trying to maintain some kind of order among the chaos, a routine. But what for? There's nothing left."

"But I can't guarantee your safety, Rob, because I just don't know what will happen if we catch him."

"Dave, I'm consenting to this, you're not forcing me."

David's dubious. "I just want you to be sure. It's not much fun being his plaything I can assure you."

"I get that, but I like the idea that we might be able to surprise him. He won't be expecting it. It gives us an edge."

David relents with a smile. "True. It would be nice to knock that hideous grin off his face - if only for a moment. But the question is where and how?"

"I still think our best bet lies in the alleyways round here. I know them inside out, especially the dead ends. We could corner him."

"Assuming he's not using any special tricks when he vanishes that is."

Rob pulls a face. "If he's doing that it won't make any difference where we are, we won't ever be able to catch him."

Rob finds some paper and puts it on the kitchen table while David shifts the coffee cups. He begins drawing the layout of the alleyways using his apartment as the base point. He identifies all the establishments that back onto them and highlights the dead ends. They discuss how they can lead the Jester into them from the various locations, running through all the possible scenarios, knowing that in the end it's solely down to where he might appear.

David sits back. "At this point we're playing blind."

"Yeah, maybe, but at least we've familiarised ourselves with all the possible vantage points. At least we have a start, or a chance."

"True." David yawns. "It's late – "

"– or early, depending on how you look at it." Rob winks.

David smiles. "Let's turn in; we can do a physical run through in the morning."

"Okay." Rob rolls up the drawing.

***

They spend the following afternoon walking round the maze of alleyways to orientate David to the layout - particularly the dead ends. They've numbered them for ease and run through all the various routes that lead to them. By dusk David feels confident that he has them down and they decide to go to Randall's restaurant for a drink. Rob sets David the task of taking them there without any guidance and he succeeds without hesitation.

As they settle on stools at the counter, David observes the other patrons, including those behind him through the mirror at the back of the bar. It's busy for the time of day, but one man stands out. He's nothing out of the ordinary, dressed casually in jeans and a shirt, but the intense way he's looking at David is unusual.

They order drinks and David glances at the man from time to time, noticing how he barely takes his eyes off David. Eventually he nudges Rob, who snaps his head round alert and ready, following David's gaze in the mirror. He picks the man out easily. He leans over and whispers, "Do you want to go now, see if he follows? If he does, head for dead end number 3."

David nods, knocking back the last of his drink as he slides off the stool and puts some money on the bar. He pats Rob on the shoulder in a 'so long' gesture, and heads out the door without looking back.

The man follows.

David saunters through the network of alleyways, pondering whether this guy is connected to the Jester, or whether it's just a chancer planning on mugging him. Even though the Jester has turned up more in this time than any other, can it really be this easy after all the time parallels he's travelled through?

While taking the designated turns to the dead end, David glances back at each corner checking the man is still with him – he is. Adrenaline kicks in and his heart beat picks up. Could this really be it? Could he really be back home tonight?

A faint cackle tickles the back of David's mind confirming it isn't just a random person following him. The Jester is here.

After a sharp left turn he reaches the abrupt dead end and spins round ready to face his follower. He hears the man's pace slow as he approaches the corner and then he steps into view.

They stand facing each other.

No changes occur and David wonders how long it will take. The only part of the man's face that is recognisable as the Jester's are the eyes: deep, black, and endless. The longer David looks into them the more depth they seem to have. He feels like he's looking into a black tunnel that seems to go on forever, spiralling down.

David's head jerks back as the Jester lets loose a cackle and he realises he's been tricked. The tone of the cackle starts to ascend becoming louder. David covers his ears but the shrill pitch still makes its way through. He shuts his eyes, bowing his head under the pressure of it at such close proximity.

Only when it cuts out does he realise he's shouting, imploring the Jester to stop. He looks up; it isn't like the Jester to do as he asks.

"Thank you." David uncovers his ears.

The Jester doesn't speak or move.

David takes a cautious step towards him. The Jester's smile broadens.

"You can smile, but I'm not stupid enough to make a grab for you. I know I've got to wait for you to … change."

The Jester throws back his head and lets out a hearty laugh this time as though he honestly finds David's comment funny. David refuses to let it unsettle him and takes another step forward. The laughter stops abruptly, along with the smile.

"Not sure are you, what it is I'm playing at? Why, when you have an obvious route of escape, would I attempt to catch you?" David tries to display an innocent, open expression, but he can't keep his smile down.

The Jester's eyes narrow. David takes another step, this time keeping his movements slow, not wanting him to bolt. He can feel the Jester searching around inside his mind trying desperately to coax out some information. David concentrates on an image of himself smiling.

David watches the Jester's frustration grow: the more irritated he becomes, the more his features deteriorate. Large bobbles of flesh swell up on his face and erupt, trickling down his cheeks and dripping onto the ground like rain drops. The hideous truth of his corrupt face begins to show through. The young pliable skin dissolves, giving way to the drawn, paper-thin film that covers the Jester's skeletal head.

Despite having witnessed this a couple of times already, it still makes David want to retch. He resists the urge to step back. He even forces himself to take another step forward, closing the gap between them, causing the Jester to glance behind him and prepare to run.

But right on cue the sound of footsteps reaches them. David prays it is Rob.

Upon hearing the footsteps the Jester stiffens, his putrefied grin faltering. At first, anger flashes in his eyes but then it dissipates as Rob comes into view, standing behind him, blocking his exit.

His effeminate tone cuts the air as he speaks, "Clever, David, very clever."

He starts to back up against one of the walls, maybe thinking of edging his way out, but Rob flanks him.

David finds it hard to believe they have actually caught the Jester and feels himself holding back a little to savour the moment. But when Rob gives him a questioning look, he replies with a sharp nod and they both leap forward seizing an arm.

The Jester's startled by the dual movement and attempts to move back, but there's nowhere to go and little time to react as everything starts to swirl around them.

Chapter 9 – Changing the Rules

When David opens his eyes he can't see anything and he can't move. He tries shifting his body round but realises he's in an enclosed space. He tries to stifle feelings of panic and thumps hard on the walls around him. All are brick except one. The more he hits it, the more it rattles. He wonders if it's a door. He runs his fingers over it and finds a vertical seam and follows it until he finds a fastening of some kind. He fiddles with it trying to picture it in his mind until he hears a click.

As the door swings open he falls out onto the floor. He must have been on a shelf of some sort, maybe inside a cupboard, but as there is no light he still doesn't know. He stumbles to his feet and searches the walls with his hands, until they rest on a switch. He flicks it. The corridor he is in floods with light. He was in a cupboard - a linen cupboard by the look of the towels and sheets in it. One end of the carpeted corridor ends at a window, the other disappears round a corner.

"Rob?" David calls out, but no sound comes back.

He walks to the corner and finds another corridor, this time with rooms leading off it and a stairwell at the end. The stairs are wide and go down in a curling sweep, again covered in plush carpet. He can see light downstairs but there's still no noise. David takes his time. He's in a house of some sort – a rather stately one by the look of the expensive furnishings. There's wood panelling, ornate light fittings, and fine landscape paintings hanging at intervals along the staircase.

He arrives in an entrance hall. Everything's oak and brass. Then a voice comes to him.

"David, I'm in here."

It's muffled, the soft furnishing making it sound flat and distant. He thinks it came from one of the downstairs rooms: two lead off the hallway on either side of the staircase. He picks the left one: sitting in a large, high-backed armchair next to a huge fireplace is the Jester. He looks like an aged Vincent Price, ready to tell a scary story.

David remains in the doorway, not quite believing what he's seeing.

"David, come in, come in, sit, sit." The Jester points to the armchair opposite.

David takes careful steps into the room. "Where's Rob?"

The Jester giggles. "Yes, where indeed. Let's talk."

David doesn't like the sound of this but needs to hear more. He takes the proffered seat and waits.

"David, we meet at last. I'm astounded by your game-playing tactics and your ingenuity: getting a friend to help you! Wonderful! I hadn't anticipated that. It was an interesting way to be caught."

"If I caught you, how come I'm not home?"

"You don't like the house, David? I've always found it rather comfortable, it meets all my needs. We must embrace all the good places, they're far and few between on our travels."

"I didn't expect there to be any more - I caught you." David feels his temper rising; he's had enough.

"Yes you did, but humour me a little, David, because in fact you cheated."

"What?" David is flabbergasted.

"Only you were meant to catch me. You weren't supposed to bring in other players. Although I'm not knocking it, it's good for me to have a new challenge." The Jester gives a warm chuckle. It sounds strange to David's ears.

"New challenge? What are you talking about?" The Jester is talking in riddles.

"You don't expect to pull a stunt like that and get away with it, surely?"

David opens his mouth to speak, but no words come; he's stunned.

"I can't have all of you trying that now, can I? No. So I have to devise a new strategy, a new game if you will, and now with two players."

David's confused. "I don't follow?"

"You want to know where Rob is, David? Then you have to find him. That will get you your ticket home."

"What? Is he here somewhere? In this time?"

The Jester shrugs. "Who knows? He probably doesn't."

This time when the Jester laughs his cackle returns, escalating to its piercing crescendo. David clamps his hands over his ears and fears for the glass in the windows. He shuts his eyes until it stops. When he opens them the Jester is gone.

David waits for something to happen, but nothing does. He expects to be thrown into another time parallel to start the hunt for Rob, but instead he sits staring at an empty armchair. He recalls the Jester saying: 'embrace all the good places, as they are far and few between' and wonders if this might be one of them.

He stands up and takes a walk round the house, switching lights on as he goes. He leaves them on in an attempt to brighten up the place and keep out the darkness that creeps at its edges. Each room has its own feel: the lounge with its comfortable soft furnishings and warm, embracing hearth; the dining room with its stately dark wood table and ten straight backed chairs, and the kitchen with its open space and island in the middle inviting a person to cook.

David pauses in the kitchen. It's been hours since he's eaten. He goes over to the cupboards and looks through them. He finds all the crockery and glassware he might need, as well as all the cleaning stuff. He's about to wonder if there is any food when he opens double doors to a treasure trove of dried goods, but the 'pièce de résistance' is the door that opens to reveal a fridge. It's stocked with all sorts of food: condiments, meats, cheeses, as well as fruits and vegetables. He's tentative at first, unsure if it's fresh, but when he discovers it is, he gorges on it until he reaches bursting point.

Before his binge, David had spotted another door leading out of the kitchen, and now, in his satiated state, it's time to investigate where it leads. It opens into an enormous two storey oval room. Wood panelling covers the walls of the lower level, displaying an array of paintings and sculptures on recessed shelves. On the upper level there's a gallery containing an extensive library of books that runs round the walls, topped with a high domed ceiling. It's accessed by a spiral staircase on the left side of the room. On the far side is a stout oak desk, and in the middle a sofa with two armchairs facing another large fireplace set into the right sidewall.

David plans to inspect the contents of this room, in particular the books in the gallery, but before he's even half way in the room he stops dead in front of one of the paintings, and has to remind himself to breathe.

It's a watercolour showing two women walking in the countryside. Their backs to the painter, they're walking away from him. They look conspiratorial with arms linked and heads leaning in to each other. One is tall and blonde, the other is shorter with brown hair, and both are wearing their long hair in plaits that trail round over their shoulders to the front. The landscape depicts rolling hills, tall trees, and even a river to the far right. All are painted in exquisite detail, but it isn't any of these things that strike David, it's what he sees on the exposed skin at the nape of their necks: a tattoo.

He can see the tip of the feather and the fluttering birds rising out of it. Someone else might not be able to make out that detail, but he knows it because he's run his finger over it many times – at least on the blonde - Isabella.

David recalls the day he'd found out Annie had an identical tattoo. She'd popped round to visit Isabella and bent down to retrieve something out of a cupboard. Her hair had fallen aside and revealed her neck. Annie had blushed when David had asked her about it, and looked at Isabella, exchanging a glance that only now began to make sense.

It couldn't be a coincidence that this painting is here, in this house the Jester frequents. It has to be them. David scans the other paintings, but they aren't in any others. He wonders who painted it. Was it the Jester? And whose house is this anyway? Does it belong to him? Is this their childhood home? What are they really to him?

David's head spins with a thousand questions. And then the room spins. He thinks it's tiredness at first until the familiar sensation of floating arrives and everything around him fades. It's time for the next adventure to begin.

Chapter 10 – Welcome to The Game

When Rob grabbed the Jester with David, his mind swooned and everything went dark. It felt like his body was spinning in a void, his limbs flailing in all directions until something solid arrived under him followed by the crunch of leaves.

He begins to shiver, the air around him cold and damp. Unable to see anything in the darkness he curls up into a ball. He can hear the sound of his own breathing. It resonates through the air around him. There are faint shuffling and fluttering sounds but nothing distinctive. He has an idea he's in a wood or forested area, but he can't be sure. He rocks himself to keep warm while he waits for daylight to break. When it does, it's slow and muted. A low mist hangs in the air.

Rob stands up and looks around confirming that he is in a wood, but the question is, how big? And is he alone? He cups his hands and shouts, "David!" But his voice doesn't reach far in the damp air. He starts walking. It's hard to discern a path through the trees with the thick foliage underfoot, so Rob heads in the direction from which the strongest light comes, with the sun being obscured by the trees and mist.

Rob continues on for what could have been minutes or hours, he doesn't know. He pauses every so often and calls out for David, waiting for any sound to come back, but there's nothing besides the odd bird call or scurry of an animal.

Rob speeds up as the trees start to thin out, until they open into a field enclosed by woodland. The grass is waist high, but he thinks he can make out something in the middle, something pointed like a hat. He runs out into the grass hoping it might be a person. But when he reaches it he finds it's only a stuffed effigy that might have once been a scarecrow. In his frustration he kicks it, intending to send it flying into the air, but as his foot makes contact it comes alive, the head turning and emitting a loud cackle.

Rob lets out a yell and leaps back in fright, the laugh ringing in his ears as it echoes off the surrounding trees. Rob can make out a pair of eyes in the man-made face and steps back further.

"Don't be afraid, Rob, I won't hurt you," it says.

"How do you know who I am?"

"There's no time for pleasantries, Rob, you need to get with the game."

"Game? Who are you - or what are you?"

The Jester lets loose another of his cackles, the stuffed body shaking with the vibration of it. "What indeed! I'm your friendly Jester, here to play the game. Come now, Rob, no time to dally over names, time's running out - or should I say this time is running out and you need to play catch up."

"I don't understand."

"Of course you don't, that's why I'm here, but aren't we missing someone?"

Rob frowns. "Do you mean David?"

The Jester's laugh is heartier this time. "Oh you're so quick Rob, it astounds me. Yes, David, but where is he?"

Rob's scowl increases and his hands clench. "Tell me whatever it is I need to know so I can get out of here."

"Oh Rob don't be so impatient. There's nothing for me to tell, you're the one that has to find him. Is he here? Or will he be there? You need to use your intuition. But chop, chop, there's not much time left."

Before Rob can speak again the Jester claps his makeshift hands and Rob feels his mind spin as the ground shifts beneath him.

Chapter 11 – Old Friends

David waits for his eyes to adjust to the dark surroundings as he orientates himself. He can see the city across the road, and although it has deteriorated further he's grateful he's in a place he recognises. Rob's flat isn't far, just a couple of streets behind the block in front of him. It won't take long to reach it.

From the dried-out park he's standing in, David observes the streets. Most of the buildings are boarded up and there are small ground fires burning: Some in the dusty bowl that had once been the city's favourite recreation park behind him, others in the middle of the street. There aren't any people around, but he can hear screaming to his left and the sound of people running.

Not wanting to be seen, he leaves the park, jogging across the street in front of him and entering the network of alleyways. He tries not to think about how dangerous they have probably become since the last time he was here. He doesn't like taking undue risks, especially when he doesn't know whether Rob will actually be at the flat, but at the same time he can't think of a better place to start; finding Rob has become his new goal.

There are shouts a few alleys over. David wants to avoid any confrontations, so he ups his pace, detouring round the disturbance as best he can, the map Rob had drawn for him still imprinted on his mind. He wants to get behind closed doors as soon as possible. He passes several people, and even sees two guys beating another, but he doesn't stop – jeopardising his own life would be foolish.

The wooden door giving access to Rob's courtyard has been kicked in and David comes to a halt, stepping through with caution. When he climbs up the metal staircase to Rob's backdoor, he's relieved to find it intact, although it isn't locked when he tries it. He steps inside.

The place is in full dark, but the litter underfoot tells him it's been ransacked. He shuts the door behind him and bolts it top and bottom to be on the safe side. In the hallway he tries the light switch. Only one bulb shines out, but it's enough for him to see his footing as he walks through the door on his left. The lights in the lounge fail despite him flicking the switch back and forth, and he shuffles to a standing lamp having better luck there. The warm glow sheds light on the turmoil in the room; piles of the debris mar what was once a warm and welcoming place.

He calls out, "Rob?" His skin prickles when the soft sound of weeping reaches him. He turns round, unsure of its direction, until a shuffling behind the broken sofa clarifies it. He stands tense waiting for someone to emerge. He calls again, "Rob?"

He hears a cracked voice reply "David?" and he rushes over, concerned that Rob is hurt. But it isn't Rob.

"John? Oh my God, John? Is that you?" David's filled with a mixture of elation and despair.

"Oh David, yes it is, I can't believe it, is it really you?"

John stumbles into David's arms, weeping as he grips his friend's shoulders with no intention of letting go.

"Oh David, it's so good to see you. Did Annie send you? Is she here with you?"

A chill passes through David as he pulls John away, looking him in the face. "Annie, John? Was she here? Was she with you?"

David searches John's grimy face, registering the cuts and swellings, only imagining what he must have been through.

"Yes, she found me in an alleyway near here where they had dumped me. She brought me here, told me I would be safe. She smelt so good, David, there were even flowers in her hair."

"Dumped you? Who dumped you, John?"

David's question causes John's face to crumble and he let out a sob as he tries to gather himself to speak.

"I don't know who they were, but they wouldn't let me go. They kept dragging me with them and using me as a punch bag. I don't know why, I don't know what I did!"

Tears wash away more words as John begins to sob. David embraces him, patting his back and making soothing sounds. He reassures John that it's over and everything will be okay now.

Meanwhile, David's mind races: how will he get them out of this? How will he find Rob? The danger outside is palpable — now he's heard John's tale he doesn't want to risk either of their lives. But he wonders why Annie brought John here if not for David to find him. David considers staying put, Rob will no doubt make his way here too — if he's in the same time as David.

As he continues to pat John's back the light in the room shifts. A glowing light streams through the hall through the glass in the back door, reflecting and flickering off the walls. Then they hear screaming, which grows in volume as it draws closer.

John and David pull away from each other and listen. David can hear words now and his stomach clenches when he recognises the voice. He rushes towards the noise. Through the cracked panes of glass in the back door he makes out a group of men running through the alleyways towards the courtyard. Their journey is lit by some kind of flaming torches. They're chasing someone, trying to grab hold of them, and it's this person that's screaming.

David's eyes widen and he hastens to unbolt the door, the sudden rush of adrenaline overriding his fear.

"What is it David? What are you doing?" John panics when he sees David intends to go outside, and grabs his arm in an attempt to restrain him. David shakes it off, only giving one word as he swings the door open: "Rob!"

David flies down the stairs, hearing the clatter of John's footfalls behind him. Screaming words fill the air, shouting his name.

"David! David! Where are you?! Help me! PLEASE help me! Someone PLEASE!"

David responds, "Rob! Here!"

When David reaches the bottom, the crowd behind Rob is closing in. David can see Rob's clothes are dripping wet, his hair stuck to his head. He sniffs the air and a sick realisation of what they're planning fills him – they're going to set Rob alight.

David runs to Rob, hoping to reach him before the men, but one of them hurls a torch, the flame flaring in the breeze as it catches the back of Rob's shirt. Within seconds flames engulf his back and set light to his hair. Rob pats his head frantically, trying to put the flames out as he continues to run towards David. His hysterical cries cut the air as his hands catch light.

A cheer goes up and the men applaud, slapping the thrower on the back as they turn and run off, no doubt to hunt down another victim.

Rob is on fire, his ear-splitting screams reaching new heights. David hears another voice join them, his nostrils flaring in disgust as he recognises the Jester's cackle.

While David stands transfixed by the sound, John pulls off his trousers, the only clothing he has available, and swats at the flames on Rob, attempting to dowse them. Rob sinks to the ground, his screams subsiding into sobs as John succeeds. John crouches down next to him to continue patting and make sure everything is out.

David grasps the opportunity and crouches down too, only thinking of getting Rob back to his own time to a hospital. He puts an arm round John and gently places a hand on Rob's shoulder hoping it will be enough.

The second he does the Jester's cackle ceases and everything around them shifts, shimmering into blackness.

Chapter 12 – Aftermath

David walks down the identical corridors of the hospital, all gleaming and bright. Having searched for Rob's room in this blind maze several times now, it's getting easier. Rob's doing well; everything's healing as it should. He has third-degree burns on several parts of his body, but despite extensive scarring the doctors think he will make a full recovery. David's relieved Rob hasn't lost any limbs and still has his sight, which had been touch and go at the beginning. No one has asked any questions about who Rob is or where he's come from; they only care about his survival. Any attempts to explain or to put into words what has happened are met with a wave of the hand – people are only glad they've returned.

Many people hadn't expected to see them again. A lump still forms in David's throat when he thinks about his mother and her tears of joy. John has experienced the same, although his state of mind is still shaky after what he's been through. He doesn't seem to comprehend what has happened, disagreeing with David that Annie was a part in it.

"Why would she? We loved each other. She was clearly part of that guy ... the Jester's game too. She's as much a victim as me."

David finds it hard to argue, mostly because John could be right, although his gut tells him otherwise. There's more to Annie and Isabella than either of them know. David hasn't forgotten the painting in the library, and he also hasn't forgotten the photo of the woman his uncle spoke about. David knows he hasn't even begun down the rabbit hole of truth behind all this, but for now all that matters is that they are back. David and John have hung out every day since, like they're teenagers again. It's been good to reconnect. They both need it.

When David reaches Rob's room, he finds him sleeping, so he sits quietly in the armchair provided and lets the noise of the day filter through his mind. The exhaustion he feels is undeniable. People keep telling him to rest and take it easy, but he can't. He has to keep busy while he tries to process everything that has happened. He has to distract himself from the rage that comes whenever he thinks about the Jester. He has to try and quell the constant questions that pop into his mind about Isabella and her connection to the Jester. And he has to stop feeling so damn stupid for not having realised she was a catalyst before they had gone.

David concentrates on Rob instead, and getting him registered as a citizen. It isn't often other people are brought back from other times but it's not unheard of, and everyone so far has been nothing but supportive.

David looks at Rob's sleeping figure with his face all wrapped up, and thinks about all he has been through since meeting David - or all that David has put him through. If it hadn't been for David, Rob might still be in his own time, out at a nightclub or hanging out at Randall's restaurant where they met. Now, every time he wakes he's in terrible pain, even though he tries to hide it and make out it isn't that bad. Rob has shown incredible strength of character and that humbles David. It also makes him refuse to be consumed by guilt – it won't help Rob. Instead David uses his frustration to fuel his efforts to support Rob and be there for him.

It was John who summed it up for David: "It seems that the Jester has made Rob pay for being a friend and helping you. How can you reconcile that? It's not like you'll ever be able to retaliate."

David knows he's right, but part of him would love a chance to try.

The Truth

They walk along the beach soaking up the colourful rays of sunlight, watching the tinted waves throwing up pink and purple spray in the late afternoon hue. David can't remember a time when the sky looked any different, but his mother can.

"You don't think he'll return, do you?" David asks his mother.

Her stride doesn't falter, she keeps her eyes on the water when she replies, "Not now, no."

"And you don't think you're being a little unfair? There's still a chance."

She glances at David. "That might be so, but I can't keep living like this; I can't keep waiting and hoping."

"But I returned."

"Exactly."

David frowns. "What do you mean?"

"You came back. Many have come back, but he hasn't. I have to accept that he won't."

"But if anything, it should give you renewed hope. If I can play the game and return, then so can he."

His mother smiles at him, her eyes full of pride and sadness. "I love that you still think your father could return, David, but we don't set the time limits for nothing. You came back within them - as did the others. No one has ever come back outside of them."

"That's not true, what about John?"

She gives a light laugh. "But you found him, David, that's the only reason why he came back. You found him and brought him back with you. Do you really think he would have managed it alone?"

David gives her a side glance. "No, maybe not. He was weak, both physically and mentally. He would have stayed where he was and probably died there."

"So what makes you think your father would be any different?"

David sighs. He wants to provide all sorts of reasons, but he can't be sure of any of them.

"For all we know he's already dead. We have to consider that, however hard it might be."

"I know mum. I just don't want to believe it."

"I know. But I'm just grateful that you made it back." Her eyes sparkle with love as she puts her hand on his arm.

He looks ahead at the beach and swallows hard before he says, "I thought about trying to go again."

She stops walking and pulls his arm back to bring him to a stop too. "No David, you mustn't! And how could you? You don't get to choose to go, he chooses you."

The warmth in her eyes has gone, replaced by fear. David sees how much she's aged in the short time he's been away. But he persists. "I think he would take me again. I think I could get him to play with me again. He told me how impressed he was last time. And this time maybe I could search for dad."

"But you could be gone forever, David. What if you never find your father? Or worse - what if the Jester changes the rules? You've seen what he's capable of."

David knows his mother is right, but he misses his father; he wants him back. David lifts his head to the dome in the sky over their heads. "Well then maybe I can do something about that."

His mother smiles at him again, her softness returning. She puts her hand to his cheek. "Oh David, you can't do anything about that, that's for our safety, for our protection. The Jester had to create that after destroying everything else with the game."

She can see that David doesn't understand. "He destroyed the worlds with it, David, don't you understand? He messed up the time parallels, pushing too many people through again and again. He destroyed the very fabric of our existence. And, as he wants to keep his toys - his 'pool of players' – he had to create a place that's safe for us, so he created this," she waved her arm in the air as though introducing the sky, "our own little bubble of time."

Sequel to The Game

Do you have questions about the Jester or the girls: Isabella and Annie? Or want to know more about what happened to David and the world he lives in?

Readers have made it clear they want – and *need* – to know more, so a sequel has begun – a full length novel in fact: I plan to have 'Pool of Players' ready for publication in the Autumn of 2019.

If you want to keep posted on release dates, about this and my other novels, you can sign up to my newsletter through this link http://eepurl.com/dw7qqD

Author's Thanks

There are many, many people who have supported me with my writing, including a wonderful group of writer friends online I wouldn't be here without. But there are a few people that deserve a special thank you:

The contents of this novel would not have been created without Miranda Gammella's Daily Picspiration blog, which is sadly no longer active, although the blog itself is still there for all to read. I really enjoyed contributing for a little over a year. Photo prompts have always worked for me.

Michael Wombat, a fellow indie author, who has been my stalwart support through every step of bringing this book together, both giving it a thorough edit and suffering endless to-ing and fro-ing about the cover. I couldn't have done it without you, Wombie.

Also Laura Jamez who has read several incarnations of The Game, and loved it every time –with invaluable input about chapter placements.

And then there is the unwavering support from: Angela Lynn, Angie Richmond, and Victoria Pearson, who betaread for me, along with Marcel Groot.

And of course thanks to my husband, who allows me to sit at home and conjure up all these tales around taking care of our two children, while he goes out to work. Thanks Ron.

About the Author

Miranda enjoys exploring her writing through flash fiction, but is primarily a novel writer (because it gives her more time to procrastinate).

When writing novels, they tend towards sci-fi fantasy or suspense-filled real life fiction. When writing flash it's the darker, more disturbing side of life. Whether this is a side effect of years of reading horror, or just how Miranda sees the world, she's not quite sure, but she finds the end result very satisfying.

In real life Miranda is a Freelance Proofreader/Editor and plays mum to two small boys, while living as a British expat in Holland with her Dutch husband and two cats.

Miranda loves helping authors with their writing in whatever capacity they need – if only to put off concentrating on her own work. She is published in multiple flash fiction anthologies, which you can find more about on her blog, Finding Clarity: www.purplequeennl.blogspot.nl

You can also find Miranda on twitter: @PurpleQueenNL Or seek her editing services at: www.mkmanuscripteditingservices.weebly.com

Leaving a review

If you enjoyed this book – which I sincerely hope you did – please leave a review on whatever platform you bought it on, or Goodreads if you have an account there. It makes a HUGE difference to the author, raising their visibility online, furthering their reach and making writing future books that little bit easier.

18005434R00069

Printed in Great Britain
by Amazon